First published 2012
This edition 2025

ISBN: 979-8-9936922-0-3

EARLIEST MEMORIES

– 1866, Chinatown, San Francisco

I stared at the grey sky, clouds looming in the distance. The usual seagulls were absent. I was lying flat on the ground, my hands clutching the mud. Ah Chen stared at me fiercely; his shaved head covering half the sky. In the distance I could feel his two minions whose names I never bothered to remember. I was fearful alright, not so much of Chen's ruddy red cheeks and looming figure but the tree branch he was holding in his hand. Instinctively, I put on a more fearful face, with a slight tinge of awe and submission. As hoped, Chen's face softened, grew into a smug and walked away.

I seized the opportunity to pick myself up and ran home, angry at myself for having tears running down my face despite my excellent strategy so effective deployed to minimize self-damage.

It all started 2 weeks ago one day when I was with Old Ma at the kitchen. I was sitting on my stool munching a cane of sugar. Old Ma was chopping firewood or another with her back turned from me when Ah Chen and his minions sauntered by the windowsill, their dirty faces seemed determined, like they were on an important mission. Usually, they would taunt our old sick dog Ah Jiao before scampering away when Old Ma hurled abuses at them. Those children are bad news, according to Old Ma, without elaborating, and I would do well in not hanging with them.

But today, they weren't interested at Ah Jiao at all. Something tells me they were up something more fun. I had been ignored by Old Ma the whole morning and fidgeting with boredom. Usually, I got to help her with sifting flour or washing rice for lunch. But Thursday was firewood day, and I would serve my bottom well by not bothering Old Ma while she's at her least favorite chore. Still, sitting on a stool and not allowed to touch anything was quite dull for a boy 6 years of age. Ah Chen was always seen with a couple of minions. According to Old Ma, he was only two years older than me but appeared older because he was 'built like a water buffalo like his father; along with a temper and brain that resemble the beast'.

Since Old Ma wasn't looking, I ran up to join them; with an expectant look on my face. They pretended to ignore me but didn't seem to mind me tagging along. We made a beeline for the railway tracks whereupon Ah Chen ordered us to build a rock barrier with the railway stones to derail the train. After a whole hour labor, we constructed a respectable looking stone mound. As soon as we heard the sound of an on-coming train we ran a long distance and hid in the bushes; my heart pounding in anticipation of the on-coming destruction. To our dismay the loud and obnoxious engine rolled on by, flattened our stone barrier without even slowing down. We went home despondent, with Ah Chen repeating some curses he learnt from his father at the butcher's shop.

Soon I discovered a sense of importance in being Ah Chen's minion. Accomplishing the 'missions' he gave me and earning his approval became important to me. He seemed to know the hilly alleys of Chinatown like the back of his hand. He knew exactly which children-friendly shopkeeper to manipulate for a free candy. Amongst the unfriendly ones, which ones are careless enough to pilfer from and which ones to avoid at all cost. And we roamed everywhere within the confines of Chinatown. In fact, the only alley we wouldn't venture into was the last row on Market Lane; where Ah Chen's father's butcher's shop was.

Stealing from shopkeepers, building stone barriers on the railroad tracks, teasing the neighborhood dogs and running from their irate owners grew dull with time. It didn't take long for our adventures to take on bolder streaks. One night I was awakened by the sound of a cat 'in heat'; which Ah Chen determined to be a loud human-like purring. It was also our secret signal. Ah Chen and Ah Gong were outside the kitchen compound waiting for me. I climbed out the window as softly as I could, and we sneaked to the back alleys where the night-soil carrier was collecting the 'night-soil' from underneath the outhouses. We hid about ten yards away. Ah Chen took a pebble and fired.

The first shot went wild; above the man's head, but the night soil carrier didn't notice. We giggled. Red-faced, Ah Chen shoved a pebble in my hands. Rising to the challenge, I took aim and fired, confident my poor targeting skills would not hit anywhere near the target. The shot flew through the crisp night air and landed on the soil-pot that man was taking out. The excrement splattered on his face. Hearing our laughter, he turned. The gods, displeased with our mischief turned the light of the moon on our faces.

"Ai-ya! You useless bastards!" poor night-soil man could only yell helplessly, with human excrement on his face, dripping into his open mouth.

We ran helter-skelter, laughing all the way, knowing the old man would never be able to catch us. The next morning, after washing vegetables for Old Ma, I went expectedly to our 'headquarters', the patch of field behind Ah Guang's family's bicycle shop. The gang was already there. Ah Chen's massive frame was unmistakable. When he turned around, I froze in my tracks. His face was a mishmash of blue and black. There was also the unmistakable of rattan cane marks on his hands and calves. Butcher Chen had unleashed his brand of discipline on his son.

"Traitor!" Ah Chen yelled and pushed me to the ground. I closed my eyes as the shower of kicks and blows landed on my body and face.

It was the end of my membership in Ah Chen's gang and renewed my faith in Old Ma's wisdom.

1952

Of course, by now waste management in Chinatown has improved a little.

I am what one would describe as a contented old man. Owning a bookstore, switching from my pidgin to American English to customers, wielding the expressions of their faces as I willed, provided adequate entertainment. In the years since I moved from the valley, San Francisco bloomed like weeds after the rain. People became wealthier and with that; the need for sophistication or appear to be sophisticated. Elite cliques formed. What better way to connect at the country club to identify one's group than to read the same books? Yes, business was good.

It has been 10 years since I owned this bookstore; two miles outside of Chinatown. Without an heir I have already bequeathed the business to the Lee Family Association in the event of my death. The shelves need some dusting and some books need arranging. But who cares? Someone can do them after I die. These days I would spend hours reminiscing over Snow Mountain; greatly assisted by the yellowed photograph I have in the drawer. How foolish had I been on that day! I had almost refused to be photograph for some reason I no longer remember. Memories of Snow Mountain, coupled with a cup of piping hot cha formed an elegant afternoon.

The door creaked open and a portly man with a bushy moustache walked in. He was a frequent customer, usually dressed like a college professor and purported to be one. He never spoke a word to me. He walked purposefully toward the 'New Arrivals', ran his thumb along the titles (I just had the workers stack new books without putting them on shelves) and selected one while gingerly extracting it without upsetting the whole pile. His actions amused me as I watched him, clearly flustered and wondering to himself why should he come to this unkempt, dusty bookstore kept by a Chinaman.

"Hi - I - would -like -to - purchase -this, - please," he said deliberately and slowly; painstakingly pronouncing every word for my benefit.

I haven't had my smoke that morning, and he probably got a dose of my blank stare.

"Sensei, I – would – like – to –buy – this – book,"

He took out some money and waved it in my face.

My eyes laid on a name on the book. Steinbeck. It brought my mind back to the Salinas days with the Trasks. Steinbeck. A Germanic name; not uncommon in Salinas. For the life of me however, I could not quite place the name to a face. The book on the counter was titled 'East of Eden'. Fresh off the publisher, I think.

I sighed. Took the money from him, gave him his change and said loudly, "Tank kew sair! Pleasee come backee!" The chap left with a satisfied smile.

My mind lit up as if fueled by a hundred sips of ng-ka-pi. I reached for another copy of 'East of Eden.'

Now my dear reader, after five days of reading it with my bleary eyes, I realized the pidgin disguise of my youth wasn't as good as I thought. I was humbled by the account but nonetheless inspired by it. And an inspiration to a ninety-year-old man must be kept alive tenderly like a precious wick at dusk. I have never thought of writing down my account for posterity. It seemed a pursuit of conceit; I knew my Snow Mountain; Susan would chide me. Ah but an old Chinaman has nothing else better to do.

This is my story, the story of Lee.

To talk about the Lee family, one has to go back 3 generations; to my great-grandfather Chan Siu who was a rickshaw puller in the shantytown of Kwantung or Canton, whichever inadequate translation one prefers, during the reign of Emperor Qianlong. In a twist that would've made Shakespeare envious, this rickshaw puller with his rough manners and rougher dialect managed to win the heart of the belle of the town, whose father was the local mandarin. Truly the match was like planting a beautiful flower on a heap of cow dung. The mandarin was a grade seven official, equivalent to the mayor of a city. As Chan Siu was from a lower stratum of society, when they got married, he had to abandon his family name and embrace that of his wife's. Now either the Lee's little treasure was truly a stunning beauty with exquisite charm or old Chan simply was tired of poverty, it must have been a heavy decision for him to commit such as un-filial act. Undoubtedly, he must've endured harsh scorn from the community. I believed it was the former reason, but my father thought otherwise when he told me this story.

Lee Siu, formerly Chan Siu turned out to be a resourceful man just needing a boost in life; for within a few years, he became a very successful merchant in a diverse business empire stretching from tea to rice and was more prominent in the then burgeoning city than his father in-law. Evidently, since our ancestral chronicles only bore the achievements of Lee Siu and his progeny, and not of his father in-law's other sons. Lee Siu had three daughters and one son, Lee Ying (Lee the Eagle); his youngest. According to the family chronicles, Lee Siu died suddenly at the age of 58; from an 'ailment of the liver'. Family folklore has it that it was some sort of sexual disease he contracted from the town's brothel, or one of his four wives, which he procured from all over the prefecture.

Not much was known about my grandfather, Lee Ying. Born in the 36th year of the reign of Qianlong to Lee Siu's fourth wife, The Eagle inherited the whole family fortune and squandered it in too short a time for even rumors and family legends to take hold. And then within a short gap of forgotten time, my father Lee Kau, loosely translated as 'Lee the dog' was born in the very hut that Lee Siu climbed out from, a harmonious completion of the circle of life. Lee the Eagle left his wife and son not long after my father was born.

Illiterate and impoverished, my father and his mother scrapped a living by washing official uniforms for the local yamen. Lee Kau supplemented his income by moonlighting as a rickshaw puller, from which he acquired a strong upper body and astounding stamina. A quiet man who inherited the gentle disposition of his mother, Lee Kau did not harbor high ambitions, nor did he curse his squandering father for his hard life. Relatives who knew the family story would shake their heads mockingly or in sincere pity at what-could-have-been for the poverty-stricken mother and son.

If Lee Kau had any unfulfilled desire, it was education. When he delivered clothes to the yamen, he envied the uniformed officials, who read long texts eloquently, communicated with higher officials, ran the county by the strokes of their brushes and dispensed justice by the power of their words. Indeed, in Lee Kau's sweetest dreams, he was an educated man with poetry flowing from his lips and the ability to paint nature worthy of the gods. Throughout his youth he was inspired by stories such as Emperor Hongwu, the peasant-emperor who taught himself how to read until he surpassed the scholars of the time. Lee Kau had no teacher, schooling or money. But he promised himself he would learn five new words in a day. He didn't know how many words it would take to become a scholar but 'with time and patience, the mulberry becomes silk'

The path of Emperor Hongwu seemed elusive; for Lee Kau's efforts for self-improvement were constantly impeded by untoward circumstances. When he was fifteen, his mother was afflicted by a strange illness which caused her to convulse uncontrollably. When she recovered, she would remain weak for hours, sometimes days. Unkind neighbors spread rumors of demonic possession and worse, a communicable disease. A local Taoist priest was summoned, and upon observing their abject poverty, diagnosed a malevolent spirit possession that was in-exorcisable; brought on by bad karma. That caused them to lose a considerable amount of laundry business. When his mother contorted in a convulsion, Lee Kau would go down on his knees to beg the evil spirit to spare them, offering ten years off his own life span in return. Then the convulsions would stop. But the tongue biting left her tongue so swollen that she wasn't able to speak for weeks. When the convulsions became more frequent and the weakness more prolonged, Lee Kau's mother knew the end was near, so she contacted an affordable matchmaker. At the age of twenty Lee Kau was matched to a peasant girl from the countryside: my mother. Two years later, my grandmother died of her illness. It was said that upon her death, an ugly demon was found attached to her torso, once again fueling rumors of demonic hold over the cursed Lee family. A filial son, Lee Kau sold his rickshaw to pay for a proper burial. Unfortunately, that meant he lost his only means of income. Not unusual for poor youths in those days, he had earlier got into debt in order to pay for the wedding, modest as it was. And now they became bad debts that he could never hope to pay off.

It was during this harsh time when I supposed life for him could not be any worse, that Lee Kau sold himself to 'Golden Mountain;' or San Francisco' where the streets were literally paved in gold. The payment for Lee the Dog's future was ten talents upon signing, and three talents per lunar month thereafter, payable annually within a 10-year contract. It was the best deal he could find, for competition was not short amongst the coolie-recruiters that littered the docks of Kwantung in those days.

The journey to Golden Mountain was the longest journey in his life. Surrounded by sea on a ship with about one hundred men, Lee Kau became extremely homesick. To compound upon his sorrows, he realized he had not even learned enough words to express his grief for posterity. On the tenth day of his journey, after two fellow travelers died onboard and was unceremoniously thrown overboard, Lee Kau was overcome by loneliness and contemplated suicide. Just then the ghost of his mother appeared in his dream, looking fierce and chided him for even thinking about terminating the family line. And behind the ghostly apparitions of his mother, Lee Kau saw a glimmer of his wife's shadow. That ended all suicidal ideations. Nonetheless, the traumatic emotional journey no doubt exacerbated his seasickness, leading to a lifetime fear of the sea. Shortly after he arrived at the Golden Mountain, my father was bundled up with other Chinamen to work the railroads, where exactly, I don't remember. In a tearful romantic twist, he discovered the young bride he left behind had disguised herself as a man on board another galley. I am convinced that very tale alone warrants a book that supersedes this one. But Lee Kau kept the romance of his life deep within the recess of his heart. All I can be sure of was thence husband and wife renewed their pledge to live and die together. Of course, I could only imagine the toll of burden of shielding his wife from the harsh environment and woman-hungry men of his own ranks. The façade didn't last long; especially since my inconvenient presence in her abdomen became more apparent.

After two months at a slave-work camp; on a warm moonless night, my parents fled the work camp, hotly pursued by the foremen. They spent three nights on the run, with nothing but the clothes on their backs. My father carried his very pregnant wife under the scorching desert sun, hobbling on a broken leg; cursing the ancestors and the golden mountain and the gods and the rattlesnakes which hissed in reply.

I guess the curse of hardship upon the Lee family has reached its embers by the time I was born. I was born somewhere in the Californian desert, delivered by my father from the womb of my dying mother. My cries of determination to live caused Lee Kau to break his covenant to die with my mother. After burying the love of his life in foreign sand, he kept a button from her jacket, which he would stare at long into the night on occasion. My father only mentioned the circumstances of my birth once and briefly. It was accompanied by such a pained expression, drawing lines on his face that were previously unseen that I never brooch the topic again.

With me in his arms, Lee Kau followed the railroad tracks and managed to stumble onto Chinatown and collapsed in front of the Lee Family Association. There, he was taken in by Old Master Lee Tong; a kinsman whose family had significant influence in the community. It seemed this Lee family arrived at California by means of voyage to seek enterprise and adventure; not running from chaos to seek hardship. And so, I grew up in the household of Lee, in which my father was housekeeper and the Old Master's personal bodyguard. The placed referred to as Chinatown today was very different back then, especially before the earthquake. Far from a 'town', it was by a collection of wooden and sometimes brick erections in no discernible pattern or order; it was as though a gardener planted all seeds in a cracked pot and ignored them as they competed to grow in the ugliest fashion imaginable. The alleyways seemed accidental; and littered with sick people and animals. Nonetheless they were always vibrant with some sort of enterprise, be they business stalls, fortune tellers or pickpockets. People used to reside in all manner of housing, sometimes makeshift tents on the streets or nook within a shop house. There weren't many shop houses; perhaps not more than four rows but within them ran all manners of businesses, like grotesque pregnant monsters with many fetuses. Old Master Lee's residence stood out like a palatial mansion by Chinatown's standards, with many adjoined houses leading to a central pavilion. I distinctly remembered its oriental architecture and various artifacts which I was told was exactly how China looked like. In my early years, I spent my time in the kitchen with Old Ma, the family cook. She would pull my ears when she's in a bad mood. If she's in a good mood, I got to taste her special winter melon soup. Old Ma frequently regaled me with fantastic stories of Chinese mythology. Not only was she a compelling storyteller who supplemented her account with sound effects, she would also use her voice in the first person, as though they were real.

Old Ma saw the spiritual world and ghosts in everything.

All the servants eat at the same time around the huge wooden table in the kitchen; our dishes usually supplemented by leftovers from the Master's family table.

"Seong boy, don't knock your rice bowl on the table like that" Old Ma commanded.

"Why?" as the different tones of the bamboo bowl against the hollow wood created a funny, haunting melody.

"Unfulfilled ghosts of the Underworld might mistake it for their family members summoning them home and come to you."

I stopped immediately.

"You better finish every single grain of rice on your bowl, or your wife will have a pock-marked face like that."

A pock-marked wife wouldn't be good, for sure.

"Have you ever seen ghosts Old Ma?" I asked her.

"I see them all the time. In fact, there's one at the table with us now." At this the kitchen maids screamed to drown out what she might say. She just grinned toothlessly.

"Stop asking her these questions!" one of them pinched me.

When Old Da the gardener died, she was convinced his soul would come back from the Underworld after seven days. She laid out a pot of rice and some dishes for him in the kitchen that night. When Small Da, Old Da's nephew-apprentice ridiculed her, she did not retort as she usually would. She just simmered white flour all over the kitchen floor leading to Small Da's room.

The next morning, the rice pot was found to be scrapped clean, and all the dishes were eaten. Old Ma nodded her head grimly, while the kitchen maids and I were trembling in fear. And along the white flour trail, were tracks of two sets of human footprints separated by a clear trail. Old Ma explained that they were from the guards of the Underworld, Cow-Head-Horse Face, dragging Old Da with his chains to meet his family on the seventh day. At this Small Da screamed like a lunatic and left the Lee household a week later. We never saw him again.

Old Ma never married although she had a nephew whom she regarded as a godson. He was sitting for the Imperial Examination in China, and one day he will be an official, she would tell me proudly. With no family of her own here, Old Ma kept company with her ancestors, the God of the Kitchen, God at the head of the bed, God of Thunder and Rain, God of the Front Door, the minor Earth Gods, the Four Celestials, the God of Fortune, The Monkey God and she introduced them to me as she saw fit; usually so I would perform some required chore for her or eat some objectionable food. There were times when I caught her carrying a conversation in thin air, speaking with someone no one else could see.

"Old Ma, why does my chest look like this?" I asked standing naked before my bath basin, gazing in the water.

My chest looked different from other boys. It looked like it was scooped out, like a wok.

"Maybe you were going to be a girl with breasts; but halfway you decided to be a boy."

"I'm not a girl!" I insisted resolutely.

"Then why are you not getting into the water?"

"Because it is cold!"

"Sounds like a girl to me."

To disprove her, I stepped into the freezing water and sat down, watching the water rolled down my sharp angled chest.

On my birthdays, without fail, Old Ma would boil me two red eggs and insisted that I eat them, for it is auspicious.

"Seong boy, you are a year older now, remember to be good and filial," she would tell me as both of us were squatting by the river, separating beans from husks.

"What is 'filial' Old Ma?" asked my four-year-old self.

"It means being obedient to your father and remember your ancestors. Have you burnt joss sticks to your late mother today?"

"Oh chicken-fart!" repeating Old Ma's favorite curse word and ran to make sure the incense was burning at my mother's ancestral tablet in the small room I share with my father.

I would usually sleep in Old Ma's small bedroom; sharing her small wooden kang on nights that father was home late. My father was always at work. Old Ma said that father was a very important official in a past life. And Old Master's ancestor was a very able servant to him. Thus, in this life, their karma were exchanged; my father in the loyal servant role.

When I asked Old Ma who my past life was, she looked around animatedly, and finally pointed to a chicken.

"There! In your past life you were a chicken!" she declared, before walking away to the kitchen.

My father never laid a hand on me; except for one incident when I was five years old. It was the Lunar New Year. And the whole Lee household was swept spic and span. Red tapestries were strewn over the furniture and huge banners with auspicious words were hung. Everyone, even the animals in the Lee Household were in a festive mood. No sweeping was permitted once the New Year begun; in case the blessings of prosperity were inadvertently swept away. During times like these, the servants would compare stories on how the New Year was celebrated in their respective home villages in China. Those were tales of a land so beautiful, tranquil, and filled with warm and kindhearted people, gentle beasts and a benevolent emperor. I wished I was born in China too. It was a happy time; mostly because father would be home for two days. The very sight of him rocking on his favorite chair by the garden was a comforting sight.

Suddenly there was a scream in the kitchen. Father ran towards the sound and found me screaming and crying inconsolably.

They were about the slaughter Dee-dee; the chicken which was my past life. Since Old Ma told me about my past life, Dee-dee became my best friend. She would be clucking away on the ground while I asked her questions and provided the answers myself.

I kept trying to save Dee-Dee from the kitchen maid, who was holding a gleaming knife. Two other maids were holding me back. Even the sight of my father was not enough to calm me down as I witnessed the impending execution of my friend. I started to bawl louder and louder.

"Don't kill my past life! Don't kill my past life! I beg you, spare Dee-dee!"

The servants started to whisper.

"How inauspicious to have wailing and crying on New Year's Day!"

To silence me, father gave me one tight slap across the face.

I reeled in shock. My ears rang. After realizing what just happened, I bawled again. This time Old Ma quickly intervened and snatched me away to her room. There, she reached into a trunk hidden beneath her bed and retrieved an elaborate looking mirror; ensconced within a metal frame that was crafted with figures of maiden, gods and heroes.

"Now look here Seong boy, look at your dirty stained face. Don't worry, Dee-dee will cross over the River of Death and be re-incarnated. Why worry yourself? It is the circle of life, you silly boy."

And through the night Old Ma fussed over me and told me stories of the Underworld where all souls go to re-incarnate. After I was convinced that King Yama, the Underworld King usually fierce and merciless in judging human souls often exhibited kindness to animals, especially chickens, I sniffled and sent home to bed. Our night candle was still burning. Opening our door meekly, I steeled myself to not cry for fear of angering my father again. He was sitting on his kang. When he saw me, he motioned me over and inspected my left cheek earnestly. He didn't say a word but brought out a set new clothes and a set of brush, ink and paper. He ruffled my hair and said I should be learning how to read and write now that I'm older by one year. And then he proceeded to teach me how to write my name. I was too enchanted with the brush and ink and ended up drawing portraits of us together. We laughed a lot that night. Before we went to bed, my father promised never to hit me again. That was my most tender moment with my father.

And thus, after that fateful incident with Ah Chen and his gang, I ran home in tears and bumped into my father at the entrance. The comfort of his strong arms made me bawl even louder

"Ah Kau, I didn't realize your son is all grown up now." The Old Master exclaimed. He was a man who looked much younger than his fifty years. He possessed a tall stature, angular jaw and furrowed bushy eyebrows that line a pair of intent eyes that commands attention. Most auspiciously, was a scar on his forehead; the sign of the great Song dynasty judge; Justice Bao Zheng. With features like that, what can he achieve in life if not success? As far as I could remember,

Old Master was always impeccably dressed in a black silk gown, a sombrero with his queue neatly tied and a gold chain perpetually hanging from his breast pocket.

Completely oblivious to my father's discomfort, I tearfully relayed to him my sufferings. My father tried to push me to stand on my own, but I held on tightly, eliciting as much sympathy as I could. The Old Master continued; somewhat bemused,

"Have the little scamp join my children in their study. Ah Ma will set another table for him."

And from then on, as a result of Ah Chen, I became a nominal member of the Lee household. Now I'm allowed to venture beyond the kitchen and play with the young masters. There were two boys and a girl all in all. Ah Yat means No 1 the elder son; Ah Yee is ostensibly number two. The youngest was Little Peach Blossoms, the Old Master's youngest daughter. She was three years younger than me, with sharp dimpled cheeks blessed with a perpetual smile and eyes that were most agreeable; the type that tears your heart if they were the slightest bit unhappy. Ah Yat was only a year older than I am. Ah Yee was younger than me. Peach Blossoms just learnt how to talk. Ah Yat reminded me of Ah Chen; but lacked his large bulk and definitely more intelligent. Ah Yee absolutely adored his older brother and would ape everything he did.

Sometimes we would pretend to be kung fu masters and spar with each other using chopped firewood in the backyard.

One day, while we were deep in our roles as kung fu exponents, Ah Yat executed a flying kick, whereupon he accidentally tripped on his own leg and fell. We all laughed. He got up, red-faced and began landing blows on the unsuspecting Ah Yee. Just then the 2nd mistress arrived.

"Why are you scamps playing the backyard? The sharp axes and wood splinters could easily get you hurt. Get back to the house, all of you!"

Ah Yat immediately started crying and showed his mother the bruises he sustained. As a result, Ah Yee was further punished.

Old Master Lee's first wife was virtually non-existent. She was married to the Old Master when they were just teenagers, betrothed at birth (according to Old Ma). She remained in China when the Old Master sailed to the Flower State (America) to join his father. He married the 2nd Mistress in Chinatown and begat Ah Yat. After he took over from his father as Old Master, his influence compelled him to take another concubine, who later became 3rd Mistress, after she bore Ah Yee for him. Not to be outdone, the 2nd Mistress maintained her influence as dowager by producing the Old Master the apple of his eye, little Peach Blossoms.

The two Mistresses couldn't be more different. The most enduring background story amongst the servants was that the Old Master met the 2nd Mistress at a whorehouse where she was the most sought-after courtesan only the very rich could afford. An ambitious woman, the riches and comfort after marrying the Old Master couldn't satisfy her. Restless and energetic, she ran the household like a train that goes in all directions. Every day, she would have a new scheme, a plan to renovate a certain wing of the house; furniture to be moved around. The servants yearned for her to be pregnant again, whereupon she would be in her chambers the whole day. Come festival season, the 2nd Mistress would move in such a high gear that servants who weren't able to keep up would be punished most severely. All servants, young or old would tremble at the soft sounds of her tiny bound feet approaching. Their lives only eased when 3rd Mistress arrived. Fresh-faced from China, she was afraid of almost everything. The 2nd Mistress took to her role as elder sister to her husband's concubine immediately, as she was able to exert her authority easily. With Ah Yat, her position as dowager was unchallenged. Poor malleable 3rd Mistress also became her punching bag when there were no servants foolish enough to appear before her when she was in foul mood.

We the children were wiser than the servants in reading the Mistresses. When she won at pai gao or mah jong, the 2nd mistress would be as generous as the God of Fortune just as she would be a tigress from the mountains if her luck changed. Her protection of Ah Yat was with likewise ferocity. An infraction such as breaking the Old Master's precious and damningly fragile antique vases would warrant a few lashes of the whip. The 2nd Mistress would immediately reach out for either me or Ah Yee for punishment. She was never successful in getting me as scapegoat, as I would run to Old Ma, the only servant impervious to the 2nd Mistress' tyranny. Hiding behind Old Ma's considerable girth and sticking my tongue out at the Tigress were one of my greatest childhood triumphs. Her orders for the other servants to catch me would fall on deaf ears, as they collect their wages directly from my father at the end of the month. Failing to catch me, it was usually poor Ah Yee who had to take those beatings.

All said, those were happy years. We had two tutors. Master Liu looked like a younger version of Old Master. Bespectacled and never smiling, he was in charge of our knowledge in the Classics and the teachings of Kung Fu Tze. He would spend hours having us recite the Analects and selected poems of Liu Bai. A slight mispronunciation or daydreaming would be punished with a whack of the rattan cane on the wrists. At first, I was terrified of him. Calligraphy was impossible with my shaking hands in anticipation of the coming wallop, which of course came. My most dreaded lessons were math. Master Liu had no patience for errors. During math lessons, the room was quiet except the 'click-clock' sounds of the abacus and the periodic whack of the rattan cane against soft skin, followed by the yelping of the victim.

As I grew older, the cane no longer hurt as much, my fear grew into resentment, which was shared by the other young masters.

Peach Blossoms of course, never joined us in lessons. We only met during mealtimes and the intervening periods like a hollow wind upon my twelve year old heart. Her pouty lips and mischievous smile controlled the Old Master, and me at will. She would never talk to me but preferred to talk at me, like her mother did to the servants.

"Your hands are so dirty," she would mention nonchalantly when I was about to reach for my chopsticks. I looked my hands, red-faced. They were clean except for a circular birthmark on my wrist.

"Eee!" she scrunched up her nose at it.

"Dirty hands! Dirty hands!" she taunted all night, my embarrassed silence fueling her mockery. Yet in my sadness, I admired her twirling in the hall, chanting in her shrill voice and drawing attention of the grown-ups at my body defect. That night, I scrubbed my wrist until it bled. After the scar was healed and the scab peeled off, to my disappointment, the mark remained, like an indelible curse.

The second tutor was Brother Robinson, the English teacher commissioned by the Old Master. He was the antithesis of Master Liu. Though they seemed to be of the same age; Brother Robinson seemed older with his red beard and hairy hands. He had a booming voice and a hearty laugh, like a friendly bear. He was always asking questions and entertaining our questions of him, no matter how ridiculous they sounded; with off-the-hook answers.

"Why is your hair red?"

"Well, God made the Chinese people first. By the time he set about making the 'yang ren'(foreigners) in the west, the sun was already setting. So, the red color of the sky was dyed into our hair."

"Why do you have hair on your hands?"

"Because my ancestor was a great bear."

"What about our ancestor?" asked Ah Yat

"Why, the civet cat, of course."

"How about mine?" I asked

"Hmm, let me see your hands closely," He pretended to inspect the fine lines on my hand, like a palm reader. He even stroked his non-existent beard like Blind Man Kung.

"Why, I believe it's the great big ape!"

His heavily- accented Mandarin made his outlandish answers even funnier. We would look at each other and laughed. Brother Robinson never bothered to teach us anything. We conversed in Mandarin, and he would have us teach him some Cantonese.

"Why Old Ma, you have a terrific rump", he would say, in broken Cantonese, thinking he was thanking her for the tea. We were hysterical as Old Ma walked off in a huff, her cheeks blushing, her terrific rump wiggling at our faces. Classes with Brother Robinson were squeals of laughter and fun.

Dinner time was a strictly family affair. I ate in the kitchen with the other servants while the young masters dined in the hall with Old Master and their mothers. Brother Robinson would be hanging around the kitchen asking the flustered Old Ma all sorts of questions. One day, I asked Brother Robinson to teach me his language.

"Why do you want to learn English?" his eyes sparkled.

"So, one day I can communicate with the yang ren and tame you barbarians," I replied. He laughed uproariously. But he picked a tree branch and scrawled on the sand; and began,

"The English alphabet has twenty-six letters; which began with 'A'...."

Seven happy years flew by. Brother Robinson became a mentor. After six months, we spoke to each other only in English; but only in private. On my eighth birthday, I owned my very first book; a gift from Brother Robinson. News of my English proficiency somehow reached the Old Master. He had me recite the alphabets and translate certain Chinese words for him. He would clap his hands when Brother Robinson indicated that I was correct. Since then, I would get an English book as a gift from the Old Master every time he ventured out of Chinatown. Soon, even Ah Yee took to learning the language and we would converse with each other in it like a private code, much to the consternation of the grown-ups. I liked to read aloud. Old Ma would complain that I sounded like a duck quacking. I kept asking Brother Robinson to correct my pronunciations until I was satisfied.

As we grew older, Ah Yat drifted off. He began accompanying Old Master to his businesses and getting introduced to his associates; the 'Uncles'. Ah Yee and I became almost like brothers. He was kind, friendly and possessed a very accommodating personality. Everyone liked Ah Yee. They also liked to bully him because of that. One of our favorite pastimes was throwing stones at the ships far away from the harbor. It was a strangely calming exercise. As we were fantasizing of working incredible destruction upon a gigantic structure in the distance, we came in contact with ourselves. We would talk about anything and everything; as soon as it came to our minds, in Cantonese but switching instinctively to English if it's a secretive, sensitive matter.

"Do you like Ah Yat?" I asked as I lobbed a rock at a steamer about 5 miles away.

No answer. He was looking for a bigger rock and threw it with all his might that he became breathless.

"I respect him." came the simple answer; in English.

"That's because he's your older brother. You have no choice. But he has been nothing but a bully to you. Remember when Peach Blossoms fell and sustained that scar on her head until today? You were beaten half to death by 2nd Mistress. Well, I saw Ah Yat tripped her. And he saw me seeing him too. His eyes told me he was going to kill me if I told anything. I'm sorry."

"Don't be sorry. I knew."

"You knew?"

"I saw it too."

"Why didn't you tell anyone?"

"I don't know. I knew the punishment will be hard. It didn't seem right to see Ah Yat suffer like that."

"But –"

"That was many years ago. We were all young."

"Chicken-fart!" I exploded and lobbed another pebble. It made three jumps before disappearing into the murky depths. "I wish I had a younger brother like you," I muttered, staring at the distance.

"We are brothers Seong. Always will be."

"When Ah Yat becomes Old Master, what will you do?"

"You are chicken-fart for saying that. You wish to hasten Old Master's death?"

"No...just you know, when it happens," I spotted an unusual pebble, admired its polished surface and threw it towards a fishing boat.

"I don't know. My mother always wanted to go back to China. I will go with her whenever she wants to go."

"China?"

"Why not? It's our home."

"Have you ever been there?"

"No"

"How do –"

"Oh chicken-fart upon shit son of a whore!"

"What?"

"I think I hit that man on the head!" Sure enough, a nearby fisherman became collateral victim of our missile assault. He spotted us and starting raining curses.

"Run! Before he recognizes us!" And we sprinted, laughing all the way.

The year of the Fire Monkey was foretold to be a prosperous year for the Lee household. That was the year my father became ill. He began coughing uncontrollably, lost his appetite and weigh at an alarming rate. Old Master summoned a physician who diagnosed consumption. He prescribed some herbal concoction but shook his head slightly as he left. Every night I rubbed and thump his back and rubbed his chest with herbal salve, feeling his once muscular chest wall dissipating with each rub. In between heart-wrenching coughs, my stoic and unflappable father relayed his life story before my birth to me.

"Little Seong, I have no possessions to impart to you. Once I'm gone, you have to fend for yourself." he said, biting back tears. I cried too and tried to close his mouth to prevent him for mouthing such words. He brushed my hands away and for the rest of the night, he painfully instructed me in the work that he's been doing for Old Master.

The Old Master was a shrewd businessman who owned several gambling and opium dens in Chinatown. He also inherited his father's position as the dragon head of the powerful San Francisco-based Sam Hap Tong; and offshoot of an underground political group in China set to topple the Qing dynasty. It was the first of the three oldest tongs in the western world, its existence preceding Chinatown itself. The other two being Lo Hup Tong and San Luen Pong. The Old Master's father was one of the first railroad workers to California and revered today as one of the founders of Chinatown. When he was established here, he brought his only son and wife over and tutored him to take over his legacy. The Sam Hap Tong had about 3000 members; and controlled the northeast side on Chinatown from Chinatown Road to Stockton Street. Besides affording protection to its territories and members, it ran the three busiest gambling dens in Chinatown. The Lee Family Association was a social charitable front for the Sam Hap Tong. When my father joined as a member, he had to slaughter a chicken, drink its blood mixed with burnt incense and swear fealty to all his tong brothers and to obey the Tong's thirty three rules of conduct. The Sam Hap Tong identified its members by a secret handshake. My father once had to participate in the slaying of a traitor; a man condemned to 'die by a thousand blades' Every member of the society had to contribute a slash. By the time it was his turn, the dead body was like a lump of burnt firecracker.

Old Master Lee was virtually unchallenged in his position as dragon head. He was loyal to his friends, generous to his followers and fearsome to his enemies. He has provided protection and assistance to countless hapless folks like my father. The Chinatown community hailed him as an upstanding hero of the community. Like most established Chinatown barons, Old Master Lee saw himself as protector and grand lord of the new Chinese sojourners to this strange and foreign land. As his senior lieutenant, my father was privy to most if not all of the Lee enterprise. Unlike other dragon heads, Old Lee was adamantly against the lucrative drug trade. Any followers found indulging or trading in opium would be ejected from the Sam Hap Tong. My father predicted that the Lee household would fall apart after this generation and I should prepare to fend for myself.

Since he became ill, I always feared my father might die in his sleep. Sometimes I would dream that he had and I was all alone in the world; and the loneliness was so fearsome I would wake up drenched in sweat. Then I would walk over to my father and put my ear to his chest.

"I am not dead yet, son" followed by an uncontrollable bouts of cough. I would then silently retreat to my bed, in relief and trepidation. Despite my father being virtually bedbound by now, Old Master generously allowed us to continue living in the servants' quarters. One summer night, the air was heavy and there was an inexplicable horde of flies everywhere. Old Ma said that flies were a good omen and portend good tidings. That night, my father and I chatted about the future, as I rubbed his back. It was the first time we talked about the future. His words to me were:

"You use the money I've saved up to get yourself a nice bride. I'm tired now. Let's go to sleep." And then he coughed harshly, the harshest I've ever heard.

One morning, I woke up before the crack of dawn as usual to the cacophony of horse-drawn carriages passing by; our living quarter towards the south-west of the pavilion is adjacent to a main road with heavy traffic. As usual, I made sure the altar to my late mother is cleansed and the incense refreshed. Then I went to the kitchen and poured a boiling kettle set by the ever-trusty Old Ma into a wooden basin. Then I mixed it with water from a porcelain tank which collects rainwater. I dipped my finger in it to make sure the mixture was tepid.

"Papa, time to wash your face."

No reply. My father has always been a light sleeper. My heart raced.

"Papa."

His fingers were blue and stiff.

A feeling of creeping loneliness enveloped me. And a single tear fell. The next emotion that followed was a serene calmness. The inevitable and fearsome ending has occurred. And it was not so scary anymore. After six months of suffering, Lee Kau has joined his ancestors. An aloof, depressed and stern man; he was always tender to me. He was my only flesh and blood and now I am the sole carrier of the Lee name. Old Master made arrangements for my father's cremation and declared his house will always have a spot for me, in recognition of my father. I remembered it was on a chilly January morning that I placed my father's ash urn in the Lee Association Hall and kowtowed three times. On my way home, it snowed.

The year of the Rooster started off with a killing.

A white man was found dead in Chinatown; murdered with a hatchet. Rumor has it that it was a crime of passion. The press screamed for justice and editorials called for more 'control' of the Chinese. The local Chinatown press advised all business to close and people to stay indoors whenever possible. Both the white mob and police went berserk. Businesses were harassed daily, gambling dens raided by the police and there were sporadic mob violence; including the beating up of a Japanese diplomat mistaken to be Chinese. The Tong leaders had meetings every night at the Master's main hall. They would bicker and argue, sometimes to the brink of fistfights. The Old Master would be the ever-calm arbiter, and the night always ended with the triad leaders sipping the last of their tea and taking their leave from the Master politely. They each wanted a scapegoat to placate the whites; as long as it's not their own kinsmen or someone under their protection. It was hard in those days to find a Chinese in foreign soil who was not affiliated with the tongs. Either purely voluntary or driven by circumstances, a 'sojourner' would likely end up in a tong. If you wanted to work for a work gang, only the tongs had the necessary connection, acting both as snakeheads and union leaders. If you had some means and wished to set up your own business, the triads were the only ones who can expedite the processing and provide 'protection'. Incidentally, businessmen who refused the tongs' services inevitably find 'random' acts of vandalism directed at their shops, until they pay up. And if you're at the lowest rung where you were tied to a white devils' railroad gang, after a long days' work the gambling and the women to take edge off the unpleasantness of life were controlled by the tongs as well. The wise thing to do was to smooch up to the tongs bright and early. I don't remember exactly the solution to the problem of the dead white man. But the tong leaders stopped coming one day. And the following morning, a dead body of a Chinese man was hung from the arch of Chinatown; lynched by a mob, and the dead white man's soul was appeased.

After that incident, a change overcame the Old Master. He would stare into space for unnaturally long periods, leading to significant discomfort for everyone in the room. Most tangible of all was his purposeful gait became slow and shuffling. Old Master was a man who commanded obedience with his soft-spoken voice. But these days, his voice became ever so soft; it was as though he lost his voice box. His wives thought the recent stress has overwhelmed him; and ordered the kitchen to provide a menu of body-energizing herbs. Old Ma thought the Old Master saw the spirit world like she did; and went into shock, as 'not everyone can comprehend the Third Eye,' she noted sagely.

In order to reverse the various adverse events that occurred in the Lee Household, the fortune teller Blind Man Kung proposed an auspicious event to drive away the gloomy aura which shadowed the house. It was then decided that that auspicious event would be Ah Yat's wedding. The bride was selected from a catalogue of available girls of similar stature and background. The necessary dowry was decided upon and sent. After that, naturally, Blind Man Kung was consulted on the most auspicious date to hold the big day.

2nd Mistress was a like whirlwind around the house. Every floor, wood panel, ornament was scrubbed and polished. Everyone had to wear their best clothes with the auspicious red color. Those who did not possess a red garment were banned from the dinner. The wedding dinner was one of Chinatown's grandest affairs. Special ingredients and chefs were sent from China. All the dragonheads in Chinatown and their clans were invited. So many tables and chairs were hastily assembled to accommodate the many guests; they spilled in three adjoining streets.

Before the wedding dinner was the tea ceremony, an elaborate event when the bride and groom would pour and serve tea to the respective families' elders, while accepting their blessings which would invariably involve some money or trinkets. Everyone present was looking nervously as the Old Master's hands trembled uncomfortably as he reached out for the cup and then into his pocket for the red packet. Nobody heard what he said in blessing the couple; probably not even himself. The whole episode seemed to last forever and was painful to watch.

Thirty days after the wedding, it was inexplicably announced that Ah Yat would be the new Head of Household. The Old Master thence retired deep into the family chambers and was rarely seen by the servants. Rumors flew that he was poisoned by Ah Yat. But the truth was never known. Five years later, I bumped into an old beggar who upon recognizing my face quickly disappeared into the crowd in a shuffling gait. The proud aristocratic features were gone. The bushy eyebrows made way for white gnarly hairs, and the piercing eyes were replaced by fearful, darting glances. But the scar on the forehead; the sign of Justice Bao, was unmistakable.

Ah Yat as a child was always brooding and would exact vengeance on his younger siblings on a long-forgotten slight. As the new Old Master, he wasted no time in making his presence felt. One of his first actions was to elevate his mother who was the 2nd wife to primary dowager status. And his second action was driving his younger brother and his mother out; true to my father's prediction. Brother Robinson was summarily dismissed. Ah Yat never learned any English.

I saw Ah Yee to the harbor. He was putting on a strong face for his mother, though in truth he was devastated by his brother's cruelty. The strong wind helped to dry his eyes before they rolled down.

"What are your plans once you're in China, Ah Yee?"

"My mother's family is in Taishan; they're rice merchants. For the meantime I will live there. Oh, Seong! What could I do? My only talent is being the 2nd Master, I will be unfilial and starve my mother," he wailed.

"Don't worry. You are an educated man. Brother Robinson said overseas Chinese are highly valued in China," I consoled him.

"Why did my own brother drive me out? I would never fight him for Papa's business."

I remained silent.

"You take care now, Seong. Here's some of my American money. I no longer need them now."

"Ah Yee I can't take your money."

"You have no one here, you will need it more than I do. I have lost a brother. Let me gain a new one today."

I couldn't argue with that. Once again, profound loneliness enveloped me as the ship that bore my only friend sailed away to the horizon.

There was no time for tears and self-pity. I suddenly remembered my father's instructions at his deathbed. I ran home to pack my things and paid my respects acquiescingly to the new Old Master and begged to leave the Lee household in my capacity as a useless servant as without the martial prowess of my father; and would not be able to assist the new Old Master in his duties.

My former playmate and childhood friend, looking resplendent in his long black robe and neatly combed hair, haughtily dismissed me without ceremony and instructed that I make doubly sure to move everything out of the servants' quarters, so I won't have to come back. I kowtowed thrice at the portrait of Old Master and took my leave.

My possessions were all filled in a small cloth bag. A total of thirty dollars and twenty cents inherited from my father, plus the ten dollars from Ah Yee, a fountain pen: a gift from the Old Master and a change of clothes. Old Ma was tearful. I hope Ah Yat would spare her in his purge. She has been with the Lee family for most of her life; even from while the Old Master was in China. She was the oldest servant in the Lee household.

"Old Ma, when I become a made man, I will come back for you and treat you as my own mother."

Old Ma just stroked my head. "Good boy, good boy. Ah Kau has a good son." she kept repeating.

The Lee household, though opulent and offered protection in a savage land; was but a gilded cage. In a way, I was glad to leave. The only heartbreaking aspect was parting with Little Peach Blossoms; whom I always fantasized would be my wife. Like her older brother, she pouted her lips and expressed no emotion at news of my departure. As I departed the Lee household, I was gripped with a grievous crippling loneliness that my gait staggered, and a mournful moan escaped my lips. I, Lee Seong, aged nineteen years, had no one in the world; no one at all.

IT's who you know

Since I have been preparing my departure for some time, I made a beeline for the Young Chinese Men Athletic Association. For fifty cents a week, I could rent a bed in a dormitory with about 40 other men; with breakfast provided. The Association was started by Old Master Yee who practiced the Northern style of boxing in the hopes of empowering overseas Chinese youth with this delicate art. Sadly, the master himself became addicted to opium soon after he arrived. He was then inducted into the labor market and was never heard of again. His boxing school was taken over by the Lo Hup Tong which wisely maintained most of the kung fu master's eclectic sparse design and patriotic calligraphy; in addition to adding bamboo partitions to convert it into a dormitory. Above us on the first floor was an opium den. Below us was a hidden basement accessible only to Lo Hup Tong's top lieutenants.

The next step was to look for a job. There were jobs aplenty in Chinatown; all of which are manual labor and subject to harsh conditions set by their employers. I have witnessed how the bosses conspired and boasted on squeezing as much from their coolies when their tongues loosened on ng kar pi in Old Master's house. I was in no hurry to sign my life away. Moreover, I detested manual labor. Anyway, with my father's inheritance and Ah Yee's money, I was probably the wealthiest; for the time being, amongst my 40 bunkmates. I wanted to be like Master Liu or Brother Robinson, men of the brush. May it be the flowing poetry of Li Bai or the adventurous yarn of Jules Verne; these works are etched in eternity in the hearts of men and the books on display. The pen could make the people cry or laugh; love or hate.

One day I walked up to a rice warehouse and pointed to a notice:

"Proprietor, are you looking for a bookkeeper?"

Before he could answer, another man about the same age as me, with a queue and dressed in a freshly tailored cheongsam appeared and asked the same question. I tried not to glare. His accent indicated he hailed from an urban town in China and his aggressive demeanor betrayed his recent arrival to the Golden Mountain.

The warehouse proprietor, a mustached middle-aged man with prominent hair emerging from his nostrils, peered at us through his reading glasses. He then handed us a piece of paper and brush.

"Write your names," he said simply. It was clear he would only hire one of us and the contest was on.

I hid my delight in noting my calligraphy was superior to my rival's. He noticed it too, but his face betrayed no disappointment or emotions. The proprietor compared both, twirling his moustache as he did so. Then he handed his abacus and a set of accounts to my rival. "Tabulate this," he ordered, pointing to a column.

I fidgeted while my rival's slender fingers flew across the abacus gracefully. The proprietor checked his sums and nodded satisfactorily. My turn came. I did the sums without difficulty, although not as quick as my rival. For the first time in my life, I was thankful to the regimental Master Liu and his spartan approach to teaching numbers.

"Well, who should I hire?" the proprietor mused aloud with a cunning smile.

"Sire, I am from WenChow Village, province of Guangdong. My family is of surname Ip. I was taught by Master Le in the Provincial School. This is my letter of recommendation from him," my rival quickly inserted, handing over a scroll respectfully, head bowed.

The proprietor seemed impressed while reading the letter. Then he looked at me, raising an eyebrow.

"Proprietor, I was born here in Chinatown. My father worked for Old Master Lee. I was taught by Master Liu," I searched for more things to say. "And I speak the foreign tongue." The old man's raised eyebrow and sneer immediately made me regret disclosing that.

"You have a recommendation letter?"

"No."

At that point, I knew I lost.

According to the saying 'Walk on foot while on the lookout for a horse,' I signed up to be a coolie at the docks. Chinamen coolies hang around the dockyard until a ship arrives. Then the foreman negotiates with the warehouse bosses for a price. Once the price was agreed upon, the dock workers will pile the cargo on the coolies' back, until the coolie said enough. At the warehouse, a foreman kept count of each individual's cargo. The more cargo one carried the more money earned.

The cargo this time was wheat, stored in gunny sacks. I had no idea how much they each weighed. We stood in a line to wait for our load. The man in front of me, who was skinnier was able to bear three gunny sacks. When it was my turn, I arched my back as I've others done to receive the load.

The first sack almost broke my back. By the time the second sack was piled on, I could not move. The third sack caused me to fall and unable to get up. Becoming a laughingstock was the least of my worries. I was fired on the spot and the word of my incompetence spread like wildfire, often laced with some pity-humor. Foremen turned me away at the door as soon as I approached. Desperate, one day I tried to beg for a chance, in a busy rice shop. The well-dressed, perpetually smiling, immaculately queued proprietor excused himself from his customers, went inside his shop and emerged with a meat cleaver and ferocity on his face. I ran in the feeble manner my legs could carry me at that time. I was so weak I did not even hear the curses he rained on me. After twenty days, my savings were starting to run low. I was down to eating one meal every two days. Unused to starvation, I decided that to stave off hunger, I should conserve energy by lying on my bunk when not out searching for work. My bunkmate at the Association would nudge me at dinner time and insist that I share his measly portion of glutinous rice. For three consecutive nights I adamantly declined. On the fourth night, I relented and ate the most delicious tears-drenched heavenly-fragranced glutinous rice in the world.

The next morning, I wandered aimlessly near the pier, considering life as a beggar or thief when I was tapped on my back.

"Ah Seong?"

I could recognize the Mandarin accented voice anywhere.

"Brother Robinson!" I shook his hand heartily. I could hardly recognize him. He was no longer wearing long white garb but in a tweed jacket and cap, just like any other white men. In his arm was a rather buxom lady with flushed cheeks and dark color around the eyes. She was also emanating a rather noxious smell which I figure was what Peach Blossoms called 'perfume'. Out of the corner of my eye I noticed we drew a few glances from the crowd with our hearty greeting.

Brother Robinson caught my look and smiled.

"I was never a priest; you know. The Brotherhood was just a teaching fraternity, and now I am no longer part of it anyway."

My eyes were still on his companion's substantial breasts.

"Oh, this is Grace. She is a gei lui," using the polite Cantonese term for "whore"

"I see," I said hurriedly pointing my gaze elsewhere.

"What did you say about me honey?" the woman slurred. "Oh! And this little Chinaman speaks English! How adorable."

"Look Grace, why don't you go back into the bar? I'll pick you up later." Her suspicious frown gave way to a grin, and she walked away. I stared longingly at her feminine shape.

"You are a grown man now Seong; sorry to hear Ah Yat kicked you out too. Peach Blossoms never really seemed your type."

Brother Robinson's tipsy frankness tugged at my heart strings. I quickly changed the subject.

"So, what are you up to these days?"

"I'm going to China Seong-y boy! The Dunham ship leaves in two months."

We walked along the harbor towards a quiet quay.

"I'm worried about you Seong," he switched to Mandarin. "Unlike other Chinese here, you are linked to Chinatown; born here; a true Chinatown-man. And with the rate things are going, Chinatown might be no more. Now even the rich powerful folks are moving to decrease the Chinese population here. How about coming to China with me? Maybe you can find some old long forgotten family there?"

"Thank you for the offer." I said, my voice cracked in gratitude. "One day I might return to see the land of my father. But for now, I would like to see America. I know it is much bigger than Chinatown out there. In China, I could find some family there and maybe I couldn't. That outcome is much worse than any I could think of here"

Brother Robinson smiled.

"I knew that's what you would say. And I'm proud you did. It's time to show the Americans what the Chinaman is capable of. One day we might have a Chinaman in the town council, newspaper rooms, or who knows, the mayor's office. I don't see that future now; but who can tell. If that happens, I, Peter Robinson can say I predicted it! You commanded English in a fraction of the time it took me to learn your blasted language. One day, you are sword, Lee Seong and one day I, Peter Robinson shall boast that he sharpened the Sword of Chinatown! There's a Chinaman in me waiting to come out, whereas in you, there is a white man waiting to emerge. Don't get me wrong. What you need to get some respect from folks around here is some more education, more than this fake priest can provide."

Those were words I remember for the rest of my life. It introduced of feeling of pride, respect, self-worth, ambition which were heretofore unknown to me. I could not keep the tears from flowing out of my eyes but fortunately the good Brother was too drunk to notice.

"Now let's see…here's what I can do for you," Brother Robinson went on. "We will draft you the most fantastic letter of recommendation that's fit for the gods. Then we will enroll you as a member of the Lighthouse Missionary Society and date your membership several years back. Then we shall search for a sponsor. I know I can obtain a list from either the Merchants' Guild or the Foreign Office. You just leave everything to me. After that, we will submit an application for the University of California. How's that sound?"

My mind was reeling.

My eyes brimmed with tears. University! My father was watching over me!

University! It was not the Hanlin Academy. Nonetheless a western university, where they store the secrets of western thought and philosophy. And I, humble orphan Lee Seong, would be the first in my family to be known as a scholar; even albeit a western one. I spent my 20th birthday staring up at the dark ceiling and saw a bright future with hazy dazzling lights.

After the spirits wore off, dear Brother Robinson remembered and kept his promise.

To my humiliation, I accepted more money from Brother Robinson to last me another two weeks. By the end of it, I was again reduced to picking leftovers vegetables from the wet market and getting ready to move out of the Association into the streets. I even picked out my spot on Beggar Alley, next to the leprous old man but furthest away from Crazy Ma, who had a habit of throwing his feces about in fits of anger. I was beginning to feel miserable again when on a breezy morning on the 22nd day of April, I arrived at the post office for the eleventh time and was rewarded with a letter of acceptance by the University of California. My sponsor was a Mr. Leon Rogers; a merchant based in New York with business interests in China. A condition set by him was that I would serve in whatever capacity he sees fit in his company for ten years after I graduate. Neither Brother Robinson nor I had met this Rogers.

"Don't be too quick to see him as a benefactor. He's not losing anything in this investment." Brother Robinson warned.

On the day before he was scheduled to sail, Brother Robinson saw me to the booked horse drawn carriage.

"Oh, and by the way, it would help that you declare you believe "Jesus is the Son of God and all mankind is saved if they believe in Him"

"But –" I was about to argue but stopped at the wisdom of his advice. Brother Robinson smiled, patted me on my back.

"Were you still in China Lee, you would've been a great scholar,"

"If there were real scholars in China, you wouldn't see any Chinese willing to live in the squalors of Chinatown," I retorted, an old habit from our interactions at Old Master Lee's. He laughed his uproarious laugh and waved goodbye.

"Good point; very good point. Touché. Touche, my Sword."

It was as sunny day. Brother Robinson's cheeks were red as beetroot not from the sun but rage. So far, we had hailed three carriages, none of whom was willing to take a 'chink' as the sole passenger. The fourth came along and the driver seemed amiable and friendly, even smiled and nodded at me. Brother Robinson warily cautioned him that I would be his only passenger, plus my trunk. The friendly driver had no problems, as long as the fare was double.

Like I said, it was sunny day, with gentle breeze coursing through the spring of May. It was my first long trip out of Chinatown. Truly the rest of America was breathtaking. We rode along a road trailing endless rolling hills towards a mountainous horizon that never seems to end. And along the fields by the road, there were white men and black men. I've never seen so many non-Chinese people in my life. My head was spinning when I arrived at the University. There were rows of neatly trimmed hedges, interrupted by carefully cultivated rose bushes. And in the distance, stood stately old buildings with their elegance; housing men of thought; and from whence the deep thoughts of men flow. Life could not be more hopeful.

To think that a month ago today, I was contemplating becoming a dishwasher for Tung Yat Restaurant!

Excitement quickly turned to disorientation. I approached a young man about my age who was striding purposefully.

"Excuse me sir, may I know the way to the main hall?"

"Beg pardon?"

"Will you show me the way to the main hall?"

"Eh?" he was beginning to get impatient.

"Main hall?"

"Mein what?...I'm sorry, I don't know what you mean," he hurriedly walked away.

Confused, I walked towards the largest building I could saw, and more people.

The other two Chinese men in the whole campus were immediately recognized by their appearances and manners. One of them was wearing a western suit but the other was like me; in brown cheongsam and a riding jacket. Unlike me, he was also sporting a queue. All of us were carrying rattan bags.

Relieved, I walked up to them and introduced myself. The western styled chap was named Chen Ping and his companion was Wen Seng. Chen Ping arrived in the California only a few weeks ago but had lived in London for a while. Wen Seng only arrived in the United States five days ago and was sponsored by a missionary in Chinatown. He had a facial expression that seemed like he was about to burst into tears anytime.

"So, where is this main hall that we need to register at?" I asked. They both shrugged.

"Let me ask him," Chen Ping approached another male student.

"Excuse me sir," he began politely in British accented, clipped English. "Will you please show us the way to the main hall?"

"What did you say?" the man burst out laughing.

Chen Ping repeated.

"Hey, Bud, check what this chink was saying. I don't get a word."

Ping grew red in the face; but politely repeated his question for the sake of Bud.

Bud squinted his eyes, and made an exaggerated show of trying to digest every word slowly

"I'm sorry. This is A-m-e-ri-ca. You needee to learnee how to speakee English, savvy?" and burst out laughing. I noticed Ping's gripped on his rattan bag tightened until his knuckles were white, and I quickly tugged at his shirt to avoid trouble.

Soon we were the only three students lounging in the area, and the sun was setting. Wen Seng asked nervously, "What are we going to do? We might be expelled if we are late." He started pacing. Chen Ping stood quiet as a statue, wordless since the incident.

Exasperated, Wen Seng grabbed the arm of a passing male student. I winced. Wen Seng has not been here long enough to understand that white folks hate to be touched like that; even by their own kind.

"Essiee sair. Wey dee mainee hor ee?" Wen Seng asked earnestly.

"It is right around this building, the building with a fountain in front," he said simply, with circular hand gestures describing 'going around' and a fountain.

Chen Ping and I looked at each other, baffled. Wen Seng was excited. "Come on! Let's go before we are late!"

At the register, we had Wen Seng register for the two of us after a similar encounter with the registrar. We were given keys to our dorm. It was the last room on the corridor, with 4 beds, a desk and a cupboard each. As were talking, the room door opened and a white man about our age burst into the room with a happy expression on his face. As soon as he saw us, his expression changed. He cursed out loud, and left hurriedly, without even packing his things. (An underling was later sent to do so.)

"White devil son of a mangy dog. Who said you were welcomed in here in the first place?" Chen Ping hissed. We unpacked.

"Brothers," Chen Ping declared with pomposity. "Within the four seas we were destined to know each other today. Let us stick together in good times and bad." We solemnly agreed. It was the most natural thing to do.

And thus we were always together. With his halting English and timid manners, the only other person Wen Seng conversed with was the minister; every Sunday after Morning Service. With time, Wen Seng told me his story:

As a baby, he was sold by his impoverished parents to a family in the city of Foshan. His adopted family treated him well until his tenth birthday, when the family fortune was overturned. He noticed that heavily ornamented family hall was becoming increasingly bare. Servants were disappearing as the days went by. One day, his adopted mother brought him to the busy marketplace and instructed him to wait in front of his favorite candy store while she visited the latrine. Wen Seng waited until sunset. But no one came for him. He grew tired and sat on a nearby building's steps; running to the candy stall periodically just in case his mother might come back and couldn't find him there. Father Morris noticed the strange boy running to and fro for two whole days and sleeping in front of his church. It didn't take long for him to figure out the truth, but it would be a whole year before Wen Seng accepted that his foster family had abandoned him. Father Morris took Wen Seng as his first convert and instructed him in the ways of the Lord and His Church. He turned out to be extremely diligent and pious.

His desire to do the Lord's Great Commission surpassed even that of Father Morris'. When the opportunity arose, the kindly priest offered Wen Seng the chance to study in the Golden Mountain. Wen Seng was non committal but would do whatever Father Morris recommended. It did not take long for Wen Seng to decide that I should be shown the 'light' and he earnestly spent every conversation to convince me to be a 'believer and follower of Christ the Saviour, not only for the Chinese but for all mankind.'

In contrast, Chen Ping was a natural leader. The son of a Qing diplomat, he was sent by his father to study Engineering and Government in England in his teens. Besides English, a little French and a taste for the good life, he acquired nothing else and was now banished by his father to harsher California until he could make something of himself. The stark socioeconomic disparity between Chen Ping and Wen Seng immediately became apparent.

"The things I have seen in Europe," Chen Ping would boast. "Iron machines and the lot. Right now, we have no chance against the white devils. The western world is way ahead of us. But the Middle Kingdom will rise again. Only problems we have are our insufferable rebellious peasants," he ended with a nod towards Wen Seng. "Even the illiterate masses of England know the importance of preserving their sovereign."

"My adopted uncle was trampled to death by an official on horseback for not getting out of the way in time. I have friends who were repeatedly slapped in the face by government soldiers in the streets for no apparent reason. The high official of my town in Foshan spent his days at local brothels instead of the yamen," Wen Seng retorted.

"Rebels always have a grudge to justify their rebellious ways," Chen Ping declared.

"The rebels of today are the rulers of tomorrow," Chen Ping quoted.

At this, Chen Ping's eyes and mouth opened wide.

"Never thought a dumb peasant could speak out like this?" Wen Seng sneered.

Chen Ping shook his head sagely. "Truly, if only the emperor knew the real poison these Westerners have been feeding these southern peasants."

I was bewildered by this to-and fro. Whenever Chen Ping ran out of arguments, he would spit into the spittoon to signal the end of conversation and lit a cigar. In Chen Ping's drawers there seemed to be an inexhaustible stash of contraband, which he generously shared. He introduced me to various forms of tobacco. The chew type leaves a lingering taste in the mouth. Cigarettes made me wheeze. One time he even managed to procure opium.

"You must try this old Seong; the seductive Temptress that our brethren has fallen for."

I hesitated. In his lifetime my father rarely spoke harshly of anyone or anything but of opium, he waxed lyrical with passion and righteous anger. If I ever touch the 'nga pien', I would be an entirely useless individual, a disgrace to my ancestors and worse than a mindless beast. I grew up imagining opium as the most lethal poison in the world, capable of 'crippling a whole nation'.

Now looking at the innocent piece of black substance; I determined that I, Lee Seong am now an educated man and shall find out for myself the authenticity of such audacious claims by empirical experimentation.

Wen Seng was aghast but before he could open his mouth, Chen Ping put a finger to his lips.

"I never offered it to you alright? Old Seong here is not a back-alley peasant; but an American sojourner. So shut your mouth."

Wen Seng looked at me with pleading eyes.

All of a sudden, I was offended by his pathetic remonstrations; memories of his persistent proselytizing and moral pontification infuriated me.

I took the finely crafted wooden pipe and inhaled. I was immediately hit by a massive pang of guilt and my dead father's admonishments. But that wasn't what I was looking for. I blanked out my mind and inhaled again. For the next two hours, I felt like a kung fu grandmaster, and could leap on clouds and execute whirlwind kicks. Immediately I clamored for more. Just then my rational mind took over and cautioned against the consequences of such an euphoric agent. Still, after the final puffs, I asked Chen Ping for more.

Sadly, that was the last of the Chen Ping's stash.

"Will let you know when I get more," he promised.

The one thing I missed the most about Chinatown was palatable food. The first few weeks I would stare gloomily at the cold roast and beans served in the cafeteria.

"You'll get used to it," said Chen Ping as he chomped on his food. "Just pretend this is prison. Anyway, it's good for you. This awful food will make you as big as these barbarians."

I glanced at Wen Seng. "You like this?" I asked, hoping to find a bedfellow.

"Too bad there isn't any rice. But I never had so much meat in my life," he said in between mouthfuls. The meat tasted bland and without flavor, the beans worse. I dreamed of Old Ma's braised pork, salty fish and tomato soup.

In the many sparring verbal matches (on occasions almost became fistfights) between Chen Ping and Wen Seng, I acted as the peace-making arbiter. But both sides seemed to see me in their own eyes and assumed my partisanship. Chen Ping and I both speak fluent English and were able to discuss things like politics in the western world, western women and English literature. From him I learnt about the world at large; and most importantly, China, the Qing dynasty. I was in awe of the ripple effects of the machinations of governments that caused my father to flee from that unhappy place. Deft with words and prose, in both Mandarin and English, Chen Ping mesmerized me with his seemingly effortless composition of heartfelt poems patriotism, eroticism and mysticism but most all, vivid descriptions of a polarized and barren picture of the strange land of China and her inscrutable reputation, which is dripping on all her subjects the world throughout like scarlet on cloth. With Chen Ping, I felt incomplete, as though my only locus of belonging is Chinatown, a much-despised neighborhood in an unwelcoming land. Most of all, I envied him for his birthright; the right to rant and praise his own nation; which only comes with an unwavering sense of belonging. I longed to belong to this ancient and crumbling dynasty. Some place to fight against, die for or run away from.

In contrast, Wen Seng warmed up to my proletariat origins and my father's ancestry from Canton. We both spoke Cantonese; of which Chen Ping could only pick out a few words. We would nod at each other knowingly when Chen Ping threw an aristocratic tantrum or went on a hate-filled rambling about the peasants of the world.

One warm summer night, Chen Ping and I were discussing whether the Greek philosophers matched up to ancient Chinese philosophers. "Well," Chen Ping puffed on a cigar after taking a swig of ng kar pi. "The results say it all. I've been to Greece. It was nothing but a collection of rocks. Yet their civilization became global. China has more than ten thousand years of philosophical foundation. We are in a setback but in a few decades or so we will surpass and civilize the world again."

"Perhaps, but the teachings of Kung Tze or Menzhi or Muzi hardly make sense here," I countered, citing my lessons with Master Liu, whose impassioned extolling of Confucian analects were still the hallmark of my nightmares.

"I give you a point there. The Middle Kingdom is undergoing some setback. The empire will rise again, but these things take time." Chen Ping with a stretch and yawn, "That is why, my brother, the best seeds grow where the soil is most fertile. Your older brother here will shelter here until the storm blows over. The scholar bids his time and shall return when the storms are calm; indeed, when the rebellious are smothered," the last part he mentioned with a raised eyebrow and mischievous grin at Wen Seng.

"You will have to go back eventually, after your studies; or when your father cut off your money," Wen Seng retorted.

Chen Ping took of his cap, and along with it, the fake queue that was stuck it. On his head was a fine tuft of hair like mine; but much silkier.

"As long as I don't grow back my queue, I don't have to go back," he grinned.

Summers at the University were unbearable. Our room was poorly ventilated and the searing heat from the sun through the window converted our hovel into a natural oven. One hot summer day, Chen Ping burst into our room and flung his books on the floor. Wen Seng instinctively shook his head. I found myself doing the same thing. Such disrespect towards a tome would earn even the First Master a severe beating by the Old Master. Chen Ping couldn't care less and he was fuming so much that he was visibly shaking.

"Stupid white devil! If he ever calls me that again, I will castrate him and all nine generations of his worthless seed!" he yelled, flailing his bony arms around. He plunked himself on a chair started to light a pipe; a futile attempt with his trembling hands. I suppressed a smile. Chen Ping's aristocratic empty threats always tickled me somewhat. Wen Seng and I remained silent, waiting for the whole story after he has calmed down. Puffing away at a pipe angrily, he continued to rant.

"So, what did he call you?" Wen Seng asked impatiently.

"That donkey face with the monkey nose Smithe jerked his thumb at me and likened me to a monkey!"

"And – ?"

"And what?!

"Is that all that he said to you?"

"I've heard worse things in Chinatown," I quipped. "What did you do?" I added, knowing the cream of the tale is at the end.

"I told him to fuck off back to his potato farm in that waterlogged swamp they call Ireland," he said in English

"No, you didn't." Wen Seng's eyes went wide.

"I did so."

I always had trouble believing things that Chen Ping said. But he was certainly capable of replying to a white man, no less a teacher in that manner. He possessed the temper, the sense of self-importance and the linguistic acrobatics to pull off a stunt like this. I possessed the latter but the first two attributes elude me. My father never disagreed with the Old Master, much less talked back to authority. As well, I should not forget Chen Ping also had immunity from any fallout.

"Maybe because you possess the aura of Tin Hau, The Monkey King," Wen Seng teased.

Chen Ping's ears turned visibly red as they usually did when he gets enraged or drunk.

"Shut up peasant! I won't be called an animal by these barbarians!"

"Then Prince Chen, pray, what are you doing here?" Wen Seng edged him with a sneer.

"Fuck you Wen Seng, you slave! You're the worst kind of Chinese. Not only do you lick these white devils' arse you actually enjoy it so much you forget what's it like to have dignity," Chen Ping's anger transformed into venom directed at the nearest target. At this Wen Seng clamped up to preserve the friendship. So did I.

Aside from inflammatory politics, the other common topic was women. Even being glaringly Chinese, Chen managed to be sexually active, sometimes spending whole nights away.

How did he manage it, I enquired admiringly.

"Just whores," he said nonchalantly, lying on his back puffing circular rings of smoke.

"No, she was not. I saw her in class today. Her father is the Rector!"

"Yes, yes a whore," he said impatiently, turning another page of the latest sleaze novel from Europe, adding further to my admiration. When he was still in his old man's good books, Chen Ping often accompanied his father to embassy parties and dinners where almost women from every color and creed were represented.

"Do you know that French women would even spray perfume on their vaginas?" he asked one day.

"How could you possibly know that you braggart?" Wen Seng interjected, looking up from his Bible.

"That's because, virgin-boy, your elder brother here, has fucked them plenty. Not only that, European women are very adventurous. They would readily open their legs to any man who's not European. And I as ambassador of our Emperor obliged them all." At the mention of the word 'Emperor', Chen Ping gave the customary salute towards the east.

"In sex, they like to move around and get most animated. That feeling on your cock is delicious. The dark-skinned whores in Southern France were the best!"

"So, you even had sex with a black woman?" I asked in amazement, my pulse racing.

At this invitation, he would grin and described in lurid detail the pubic hair of different women of different nationalities. At this, Wen Seng closed his ears with his fingers.

Although the three of us stuck together whenever visible, I soon made friends with the locals. I remember there was the Presbyterian minister Dr Maurice Thompson from the Rectory, Anselm Wayne a former missionary to China and his perpetual request that I spoke only Cantonese with him. His command of the language was so poor that we degenerated to using sign language or until I switched back to English out of sheer despair. There's also Lawrence Byrne from Virginia, whose friendship I consider the most genuine and truest. Lawrence came from an aristocratic family; with 'old money' as he described it. His family traced to some wealthy merchants and war heroes. He was about the same age as me, never met a Chinaman in his life and did not possess and pre-emptive desire to learn the Chinese culture. We met on the field one day when I inexplicably signed up for boxing lessons. Perhaps inflamed by jeers and insults hurled at me, or the encouragement to my opponent to 'down the chink' I delivered at my opponent a sharp right hook with surprising strength he collapsed to the ground, not moving for minutes, which seemed like hours as the crowd's hushed silence stung the flesh of my back. Just as I was about to imagine the real horrors of a lynch mob, my felled opponent's eyes flew open with wide brown pupils staring right ahead at me, squinted a while, and with a broad smile said

"The name's Lawrence Byrne! What's yours?"

We would meet for boxing. Lawrence and I spoke about everything; boxing lessons, food, the current railways debate sweeping the headlines in California, the utter stupidity of politicians, how there aren't enough women in campus, how to get the most taste out of the best tobacco. We talked about everything but China or Chinese culture. With Lawrence (and a subtle headgear disguise), I managed to frequent the pubs and bars of the campus to sample American life. Indeed, the company of friends adds spice to even the blandest meals. I began to enjoy the piping hot potato with skins, onions and the even got used to carving food with a fork and knife. I added to my leisure western music, performing arts and poetry by old dead poets.

Wen Seng, whose halting grasp of English and shy nature kept him close to his religious studies. And Chen

Ping who despite his cosmopolitan upbringing, seemed to be more withdrawn and xenophobic as time wore on.

"I think the salvation of China is already here, in the form of Jesus Christ," Wen Seng opined one day, as he was polishing the portrait of his mother.

At this Chen Ping bristled visibly.

"That cult is just an excuse for the foreigners to invade our country! Even the white devils themselves don't care for it in their own country. They want to make us weak and subservient to them."

"Chinese or foreigners, we are all created equal by God. And He loves both equally."

"You don't even know what you're talking about, you dumb peasant," Chen Ping pointed his finger threateningly. "Completely brainwashed by a white devil!" he added contemptuously.

"My life was picked up by Father Morris. Yes in China they are evil oppressors. But there are also good ones," Wen Seng said in a conciliatory tone.

Chen Ping was still angry.

"Alright then, your mother wasn't a Christian. Is she rotting in your Christian hell now? And your priests disallow ancestral worship, so the poor woman's soul is hungry and cold without a filial son to honor her."

"Don't bring my mother into this!" Wen Seng looked like he was ready to strike; which was comical.

Chen Ping knew he struck a nerve and looked apologetic.

"I just wanted to show you the truth," uncharacteristically humble.

"Just shut up."

Attending classes were one the most formative of my years. Mine were Latin and Contemporary Philosophy. The school administration compelled all Chinese students to take English classes also. I didn't mind. Wen Seng shared my enthusiasm with an extra dose of his own. Chen Ping was restless. Besides food, the next most difficult thing at first to get used to was sleeping on a soft mattress. But restful nights of a happy and satisfied life alleviated the strain on my back a great deal. Chen Ping would snore loudly after exhausting himself arguing with anyone who would take him on. He would even talk in his sleep; arguing with his father. Wen Seng would burn the midnight oil, repeating simple English phrases to himself. I would be thinking of the glorious day that lies ahead. My father had always extolled the virtues of education and scholarship. Now I marveled at his foresight. Illiterate himself and surrounded by men who live by the sword, he somehow understood the power of knowledge and its magnificent rewards. I could not help but compare my present self with Lee Seong of Chinatown nine months ago. How I pity him! He was so deprived and naked, starving without feeling hunger. The freezing winds of December were best spent in the library; where my soul basked in the shine of things unknown. I read every book that caught my fancy. After a few months, I was bold enough to approach the professors about topics I didn't understand. By and large they were very eager to teach. I taught myself Greek and Latin, though I enjoyed neither. There really was nothing much else to do. I never saw the point in engaging the field sports, except for that singular boxing episode with Lawrence. Without the obsidian protection of academia, the university field was as dangerous as venturing out of Chinatown. I was curious about the social events. The news bulletin always has announcements of a weekend dance or a picnic. Though not explicitly stated, I could not imagine a Chinaman showing up in any of these. Wen Seng never showed any interest in anything else except in his studies and reading his precious Bible.

Far from Chinatown, we had no idea what zodiac it was. When Chen Ping and I started arguing about whether it was the Year of the Snake or Rat, Wen Seng sheepishly produced the 'tung sing'; or Chinese almanac, a staple in every Chinese household; and a tool of feng shui, astrology, mysticism and to Chen Ping's satisfied smile, a sign of Chinese superstition. It was the Year of the Metal Snake. A year predicted to be unfavorable to the Wooden Horse, Fire Rabbit and Metal Monkey. We welcomed the lunar New Year by sharing a hot pot in the dorm. Chen Ping with his seemingly limitless resource managed to procure a claypot, some meat and even supplied the ng kar pi.

It was the last day of the lunar New Year celebrations, the 15th day, at around midnight we were awakened by violent banging on our door, on which we had installed a bolt. I started towards it but backed off when I heard 'bring the axe!'. Within moments, a sharp blade plowed through the wooden partition like paper with a loud noise. The three of us were suddenly swarmed by about 20 white males I recognized to be students. I was overpowered easily and kicks and punches were delivered liberally. I instinctively crouched into a defensive position I knew would minimize most critical injuries. Wen Seng's cries echoed across the room. I spied Chen Ping fighting back like a lion, throwing everything in sight at his assailants, even wounding a few. He lunged at one of them, caught hold of his head and started banging it with the claypot. Suddenly inspired, I started flailing my arms and legs about too, but I was quickly subdued and the blows resumed.

In the end however, even Chen Ping was no match for six men, two pinning him to the wall, the rest delivering punches.

"Which one of you China scum stole my watch?" the leader, known as James or Jim or something snarled menacingly. We had no answer. I was bewildered. Chen Ping was spiting at anyone within distance with his limbs clamped down by four men. When I glanced at Wen Seng, I was filled with hatred and despise for him. Large globs of tears were rolling down his red cheeks; his facial expression was contritely submissive. His queue was tied like a rat's tail onto the bed railings. It was a pathetic sight. At that moment I hated him more than our assailants.

All our possessions were overturned and rummaged. When they arrived at Chen Ping's drawer, they fished out a gold pocket watch which I know belonged to him. James inspected it wistfully, the flashes of greed and moral dilemma clouding his face momentarily. He turned on us,

"We are not thieving animals," he declared to convince himself and flung the watch on the floor. "I have a witness that it was one of you monkeys," he spat. "This isn't over. Just you wait."

They left. I could not allow myself another glance at Wen Seng, whose sobs continued into the night.

Since that incident, life became harder for us. We no longer could eat at the cafeteria for fear of another beating or worse, poisoning. Chen Ping took it all in stride, snarling at everyone like a wounded wolf. Wen Seng was completely miserable. I took comfort in that I was adjusting to this adversity better than him.

A week passed. And James made true his promises.

The three of us were summoned to the Provost's office. He was a bald man with bushy sideburns and pursed lips, his expression was indecipherable.

"Gentlemen, a very serious allegation was brought forth against you. A valuable possession has been stolen and there are three reliable witnesses willing to attest that it was one of you," he wasted no time. We kept silent. He paused for effect and continued,

"The Board has decided that we cannot allow such elements to permeate the learning environment in this institution. As such, I'm giving you five days to own up or the three of you will be expelled."

"Son of a flea-infested dog!" Chen Ping bristled when we were in our room. "He's been waiting to get rid of us and now he finally gets his chance!" It seemed true.

I spent that night staring at the ceiling, wondering what the future might hold. The next morning I was examining my wounds in the washroom when Wen Seng broke in and pulled me into a corner cubicle. His palms were sweaty and he was out of breath.

"Brother Lee," he knelt on the ground and started kowtowing. He knocked his head so hard on the concrete floor blood oozed from the gash on his narrow forehead.

"What are you doing?" I was alarmed. I pulled him up and had to slap him a few times to inject some coherency in the man.

With tears and mucus dripping from his nostrils, Wen Seng then confessed to me that he stole James' watch. He saw it hanging from his coat at the cloakroom. There were many people. He knew he was seen.

"Why?" I asked.

No answer. Just more weeping.

"I cannot be expelled. I will be a shame to Father Morris , the whole church and my family's name! I would jump into the sea before that happens!"

"I cannot. I simply cannot!" he wailed like an animal, tempting me to slap him again.

He begged me to help him; and to keep it from Chen Ping, whom I would not doubt would kill him. The picture of him begging me for help, on his knees and head bowed, such complete obeisance and helplessness infuriated me greatly. Just to get him off his feet and relieve my own rage, I punched Wen Seng in the face and sent him flying across the room. Satisfied, I turned around and walked out.

I never did find out why Wen Seng stole the watch. What was more perplexing, I did not know why I was filled with an altruistic desire to help him. I supposed it was to compensate pound for pound the hatred I was generating towards this wretched fellow, my fellow countryman.

Emboldened by altruistic recklessness, I walked right to the Provost's office, knocked and entered.

"Provost Block, I am the scapegoat you are looking for. Expel me and spare my fellows," I said, my anger rising with every word.

Eugene D Block III, Provost, turned around. He was red in the face. He pointed his forefinger at me.

"Don't you dare pretend to magnify this than a greedy act of theft and don't you dare tell what to do!" he shouted. I stood still, clenching my fists to fight back tears, as one would when standing in front of an execution squad.

His wheezing abated. He looked away and took a few audible breaths.

"Mr. Lee, at the time of the theft you were in my class dissecting the poetry of Virgil. I suppose that is how you people see things. I don't quite understand but I cannot deny I admire it. And...." He started pacing.

"Mr. Lee, you will not be expelled...but will leave the University for Personal Reasons. I will write a letter of support to your sponsor. Carry it with you in your future endeavors. That is the most I can do for you". Without looking up, he went straight to his desk. I fantasized on the different ways I would like to hurt the man as he wrote the letter while I stood like a statue.

I could hardly carry myself back to the dorm. Chen Ping opened the door excitedly.

"Little brother! We are being set up! So my girl Angie told me; James Thompson is the son of one the members of the Board of Directors and major donor to the university. His dog shit of a father is a low-level politician running on the platform that us Chinese should be driven out of this country..." he stopped when he saw my crestfallen face.

"Don't tell me..."

I nodded.

"But wha--?"

I was in no mood to explain or confabulate and headed straight to bed and bury my head in sorrows. Then Chen Ping went ballistic and began throwing pots and books around. I did not look at Wen Seng, who was hugging his knees.

The next day, Chen Ping threw the San Francisco Herald at my feet. "Take a look at this," he spat in disgust. The headline was:

"Chinese Exclusion Act passed." And there were pictures of white men rejoicing.

I wrote to Brother Robinson at his given address. Days passed but received no reply. Banned from class, I anxiously awaited by the mail collection office to no avail.

Every meal was taken with a lump in my throat every sunrise an unwelcome sight. I have till the end of the week. Chen Ping gave me his whole month's allowance and threatened me with bodily harm if I did not accept it.

"I wrote to my father to send me more. The old man refused to believe me- said he'll not finance any further whoring and squandering of his fortune. The old miser. When he was my age, he already had three wives!"

When he was done ranting, he put his hand on my shoulder.

"Little brother, I won't ask you why you did what you did. But within the Four Seas we were destined to meet. One day, the world will belong to China again. And I will see to it you are one of the leading architects of this future," the scion of China declared confidently.

Wen Seng came forward, the pitiful expression seemed perpetually stuck to his face.

"Brother Seong, I want you to have this." He handed me his well worn leather-bound Bible.

"Father Morris gave it to me. I have read it cover to cover and don't think I even understood one percent of it. With your command of English, you will be able to decipher it so much quicker."

"I can't take this. This is your only possession." I felt somewhat relief that now I could hate him again remorselessly.

"Don't worry, Father Ross already gave me another one." His about-to-break-out in tears expression so alarmed me I quickly accepted his gift.

Three days before the end of the month, I decided to leave. On foot. To nowhere. With no family, no home and no desire to return to Chinatown, I would to seek my fortune out west, to see what Chinese who've done likewise ended up as.

It was a full moon. An owl stared at us from a tree.

They both had walked me to the university's entrance, although I could not bring myself to acknowledge Wen Seng.

There were tears in Chen Ping's eyes.

"My brother, I'm sorry you are still a virgin." I had no reply to that.

We were squatting on the grass, enjoying one last chat and smoke. Suddenly an extremely noxious smell hit our noses.

Unbeknownst to us; Chen Ping had taken off his trousers and dump a pile of hot stool right on the hedge spelling 'University'.

"There, little brother, that is for you," he stood up proudly tying his trousers.

"For a so-called aristocrat, you are like an animal," Wen Seng said through his pinched nose whilst I ran away from the disgusting scene.

"Shut up you chicken-faced peasant" Chen Ping waved at me.

"You take now little brother! Remember to write!"

It would be many years with the Trasks that I learned to find comfort in the lonely wild country of the west in those days held for me a sense of trepidation. In my youth however, the very absence of a fellow Chinaman brought a sense of fear of the unknown to me. It seemed every step I took brought me deeper into an unknown wasteland. As the sun began to rise, I hastened my steps, yearning to reach the railroad tracks. When I finally stumbled upon it I was so relieved I could hug it like a mother. I walked southwards because that was the direction to Chinatown. It was after an exhausting, seemingly unending hike before a southbound train finally came along. I waited until the last car and jumped on the first open car. It was occupied by three men who immediately noticed my presence. They wore yellow stained beards, and dirty dark blue khaki and jackets. I realized these were probably runaway prisoners, laborers or soldiers. I groaned inwardly. I nodded with a smile and sat next to a window furthest from them. The sun was already setting. One of them suddenly stood up; I was too tired to make any defensive stance.

"Hey, What's this Injun doin' here?" his fruity breath wafted across the room to my nostrils.

"That ain't no Injun, it's a girl, Harry!" his companion exclaimed.

"How do you know that?"

"She ain't got no beard."

"Injuns have no beard too."

"An Injun girl!" the third one said, licking his lips.

At that, I casually took off my cap and unbuttoned my shirt, nonchalantly while looking outside to declare my sex while feigning ignorance. I even coughed out loud to reveal my voice.

"Hey! This ain't no Injun. He's a chink!"

"Well, I'll be damned. A chink without a pigtail."

"What are you gonna do about it, Harry?" his companions asked.

"Well, nothin' I ain't got no prob with em chinks. Welcome to America bud."

I pretended not to understand, maintained my cautious friendly demeanor and looked back out. My instinct to escape was overridden by my exhaustion. The first day had been extremely uncomfortable. I was worn out. I quickly munched on a bun and reminded myself that food supplies will only last me another two days. I tried not to think about it as I tried to catch some sleep.

The God of Dreams mercilessly plied me with memories of being a university student. I awoke right before dawn. I got up and was about to take out my map when I heard,

"Hey Nat," the one with the wooden hand asked his colleague lazily. "What do you think that chink has in his bag?"

"Nothin' of value; else he wouldn't be here"

"You never know. Think he might have gold from Californy?"

My hair stood at such talk. These men were openly discussing whether they should rob me! It took all my self-control to not look at my enemies. As I pretended to look out at the scenery, I perked my ears to listen more.

"Huh, I don't know. We should ask the Cap'n". I heard them shuffling along the plank to their leader.

By the time they turned around, I was gone.

I was extremely fortunate to have jumped off that train in such haste without breaking my leg. I did however sprain my ankle and hobbled painfully upon the merciless hard road, avoiding travelers from afar yet yearning for some company. I was not even sure I was heading the right direction except hoping the railroad tracks will lead towards Chinatown.

On my second night on the road, in a small clearing by a creek near the railways, I cried myself to sleep, hot angry tears rolled uncontrollably at the fact that they were rolling down.

The next morning, I was awakened by the horn of a coming train. I hopped on but did not venture into any cars. I just held on the railing by the side.

I could not remember how much time passed, before a lightning bolt struck my hand. I let go and fell off the train, landing my bottom on the hot rail. The train conductor was swinging his truncheon which just broke my hand. His disappearing menacing smile burnt in my memory as the train rolled away.

My left hand felt as it all the bones were broken, even the slightest movement hurt like childbirth. According to the Old Ma, the treatment for broken bones is realignment and a tincture of time for them to heal. Whenever I sprained my ankle at play, she would wrap the joint in tight warm compress, layered with some fragrant herbal salve.

I wrapped my hand up with some leaves. The only salve were my hot tears.

I had to keep going north. Having had enough of the rails, I ventured upon the road. Even with the scorching sun, the road seemed friendlier with its lack of human beings. The road was flank by cornfields, and it was the corn harvest and I easily stuffed my bag with a few full ears.

Before long, I longed for human company. Just to hear the sound of a human voice. The isolated farmhouses were too threatening. Before sunset I chanced upon a camp with a fire. Though the road was like King Yama's torture of fire in the daytime, at night it became so cold my ungrateful toes screamed for warmth and rest. The campfire was a welcome sight.

I approached the group of men slowly. I noted there were some women and children too.

A customary nod from the leader around the fire was permission enough for me to share the warmth. I greedily rubbed my hands near the fire.

After hushed words of 'chink' and 'seems harmless' and 'poor creature' passed around, the group resumed their conversation without acknowledging me.

They spoke English with an accent and dialect that was too thick for me to catch. The men all wore tattered clothes, had unwashed faces. The women were quiet, had bad teeth, and wore a scurrilous look about their faces. The children stared into space. Some were asleep.

The poverty of America was an extremely interesting topic at the University. I vaguely remember passionate arguments made by clean-bearded scholars about policies of land distribution, labor, taxation and migration. Now seeing, hearing and smelling this topic myself; it was clear the professors had no idea what they were talking about. Knowledge is not infallible.

These folks talked about the lands they left behind. The starvation. The deceit. The bitterness, regret and desperation in their voices were audible. Such discussion died out within minutes. People only liked to hear of others' misfortune if they have the privilege to shower pity. Otherwise, if it's a mirror of their own situation, no thank you.

"Ching-Chong, you wanna go to Chinatown?" The leader of the band, whose name I figured was Jasper asked animatedly complete with hand gestures.

I nodded repeatedly. Members of the group looked curiously at me.

"No pigtail." I heard amongst the murmur.

"Well," he eyed me up and down. "I doubt he could make the trip. There's a chain gang up on the road, looking for runaway soldiers, hicks, gooks, chinks, whoever they can catch to build roads for em. I reckon e goes to San Francisco."

"Go San Francisco, yes? Big Chinatown there I 'eard" he said, pointing towards the south.

I smiled broadly, without indicating comprehension. Inwardly I cursed myself. How could I have travelled in the wrong direction all this while? The other 'Chinatown' I thought I was heading to another mining settlement east of San Francisco. I thanked my father's ghost for Jasper.

"Poor chink's gonna be dead by tomorrow's sunset."

"'fraid so,Billy-boy," a man named Drew said sagely.

"Nah, this ain't right. Listen Chong, you come yonder with us tomorrow towards the south. You get off when we meet your people alright?" Jasper asked.

I nodded vigorously.

"Can't be sending men to their deaths, not even a chinaman,"

A roar of approval rose from the crowd. Someone yelled 'Amen!'

And so, after just three days on the road, which made up for a lifetime of education, I turned around towards back to Chinatown.

My broken hand seemed to invigorate my spirit. And I came to the realization that the harsh country of America was no place for the Chinaman. The people I met were piss-poor and more desperate than the Chinaman. In fact, they have no hope, no anchor and no ancient culture to dictate their conduct. Even Master Lee's most psychotic vulgar minion had an ordered way of life; a mission and purpose; for without it, he has no identity.

The members of Jasper's convoy pretty much left me alone throughout the journey. With friendly gestures they invite me to share in their meals and warmth. In return I offered to help them with menial tasks of feeding beasts and washing utensils. While on the move, I was invited to ride on the donkey cart with the children.

Unlike the adults, the children were scrubbed clean. They looked curiously at me. One of them gingerly touched my hand and backed away. Everyone giggled.

The oldest boy got bolder and reached for my bandaged hand.

"I wouldn't do that if I were you." I said sharply in English.

"Sorry," he retreated, immediately shamefaced and amazed at the same time.

"What's your name?" I asked.

"John"

"I'm Gwyn" the little girl said. "And she's Emily" Gwyn volunteered.

"What's your name?" asked Emily

"And I'm Seo--. Call me Lee"

"Why'd the grownups call you Chink?"

"Very likely, because the Chinese are subjects of the Qing government. The Qing government governs a country called China. The correct term to describe me and my people is 'Chinese '"

'Chy-nese' repeated Gwyn.

"That's very good Gwyn." That made her beam with pride.

"China is really far away," declared Emily.

"Yes, though I'm not sure exactly how far..."

"Do all Chinese people have small feet?"

"Are there any Chinese children?"

"Pa said Chinks, err Chinese eat rice all the time. Don't you like potatoes too?"

"Do Chinese people play the banjo?"

I tried my best to satisfy their queries.

Under the moonlight, with the children asleep, I planned on my survival in Chinatown.

After 2 days, Jasper stopped the caravan.

"Look out yonder. Folks told me that 2 miles down is Chinatown entrance. Me and ma folks are going further south. You take care now ma friend."

"Tank kew veli veli muchee!"

I waved goodbye. John, in his pale blue overalls and straw hat and 4 feet stature was standing on the cart as they moved away.

"Goodbye Lee. I will always remember you," John, the tallest amongst the children, waved.

"Farewell, John."

As I looked over at the horizon, the Pacific Ocean which glimmered from the golden disk so brilliantly when I left Chinatown last year, seemed so dark, gloomy and inviting now. My heart was gripped with such coldness and clarity that I felt like a soldier primed for war. And thus, I was back on the streets of Chinatown. It was surprising even to me, the development that took place in me in the last 10 months. I had learnt more on the road than those months in university. Chinatown doesn't seem so foreign now. Westerners don't seem so intimidating, and the Chinese people seemed more like myself.

I checked in at the same dormitory on top the Young Chinese Men Athletic Association and spent the night sleeping the tumultuous sleep of a condemned prisoner. The next morning, I received a forwarded a letter from Brother Robinson. It was stamped Guangzhou. Anti-western sentiments were running similarly high in China. Many western merchants were thrown out; their businesses closed and or their cargo stranded at the harbor. There were daily protests and local uprising against western settlements. He heard that in one such incident, a British merchant's warehouse was set on fire by locals. His wife and daughter were killed in the ensuing melee.

I wrote a short reply to Brother Robinson; a short explanation about what happened and to not worry about me. Sweet, sour, bitter or spicy, we must carry on in life. And that he takes care of himself in the midst of the hostile environment. After completing that letter, I felt a lot better myself, as if a cloud lifted over me.

I spent another hour thinking of a plan and then slept a fitful sleep in which my father appeared to me in a dream. The next morning, I sauntered downstairs and spoke with the caretaker of the Young Chinese Men Athletic Association that I wished to speak with Master Hwang. The old man retorted that Master Hwang is busy and I wish to become a member of the association the fee is twenty dollars per year and if I want to learn kung fu, then the class starts at the Hour of the Rooster and the fee is three dollars per month.

"Listen you old fool. I have extremely important business with Old Master Hwang. Heard of the Chinese Exclusion Act? Your family and seed depend on me!" This was the first time in my life I acted so forcefully, and it took everything out of me. Although effective, as the old man went pale and ran to fetch his master, I was trembling inside.

According to my father, the Young Chinese Men Athletic Association was a front for the Lo Hup Tong; whose godfather is Old Hwang, one of Old Master Lee's greatest rival. In recent years, Hwang has surpassed Lee due to his virtual monopoly on the snake trade; where coolies were imported from China and distributed to labor-starved local companies; be they railroads, mining or for his own personal force.

Old Hwang appeared; along with two well shirtless bodyguards; one of whom bore a scar across his face. Old Hwang was hardly the menacing old man with a patch over his eye like I imagined. He was portly, dressed immaculately in a long black cheongsam, gold rimmed spectacles and neatly combed hair with no queue, not unlike Old Master

Lee. One might even say he has a kindly appearance. An 'old fox' is how my father described him. He peered at me curiously, searching his memory. His eyes were sharp, betraying an alert mind. Although he owned most of the dens in Chinatown, Old Hwang abhorred opium. I tried to appear nonchalant.

"What can I do for you, young man? You seemed to have made quite an impression on old Lam here" he asked pleasantly. The old caretaker retreated to behind the counter to watch the unfolding drama.

"With respects, Old Master Hwang; the question should be what I can do for you."

He raised his eyebrows. That was my cue.

"The Chinese Exclusion Act, made into law last week by the white devils. I've read it in detail, in the foreign devil's language. It is a travesty to the Chinese people. We are not the only immigrant group to this land. But we certainly are the most hated. Since our forefathers first stepped foot on this so-called Golden Mountain, the locals have persecuted us relentlessly. The Middle Kingdom subject works for lesser wages, more hours and what do we get in return? The Great Qing in all its might have always bestowed benevolence to outsiders residing in the Middle Kingdom. These barbarians under the guise of civilization; instituted systematic bullying, extortion and pure hatred towards us. If not for outstanding leaders of the community such as yourself, our brethren would be suffering immeasurable toils," I paced up and down in the manner of lecturers in the university. I glanced at Old Hwang. He was beaming, seemed interested; but not terribly so, as if he was more curious in me than what I was saying.

Nonetheless, he did feel compelled to invite me to sit. Hot tea was served. I relaxed.

"You seem to have some years of learning behind you, young man. You would do better serving the Emperor back home," he began.

I held up my hand to interrupt him. I could see he was affronted by his bulging eyes. His bodyguards' muscles bulged. If he was my father, he would have rightfully slapped me for doing that.

Clearing my throat and stifling my pounding heart, I continued:

"With apologies, Old Master; the men of learning in the capital cities were the ones who allowed this despicable law to take effect in the first place. It is the real people, you and I and our brethren who will be affected by it. You Old Master, have helped thousands of Chinese seek a better living in this land. You have successfully enticed the local authorities with gold but now this law seeks to even take that leverage away."

He narrowed his eyes. The human smuggling aspect of his business was not exactly a secret in Chinatown.

"Those are just words on a piece of paper. Today is not the first days the white devils have made things difficult for me," he said nonchalantly, sipping tea.

"Old Master, with respect; you know above all others that the government here can enforce laws with the efficiency of the Great Hong Hei Emperor. The passing of this new law and subsequent enforcement is a concerted attempt on you." I was taking a real gamble indirectly comparing him with the emperor. As an ex-mandarin official, he might take exemption at such subversive words. As a warlord thousands of miles from the Middle Kingdom, he might be pleased with it.

He smiled.

"What you need Old Master," I continued now that I have his ears, "is someone who can work on both sides and act in your best interest. And that someone is familiar with the lay of the land of the foreign devils. Who not only speaks their language but understands their minds. I know you have white folks in your employ, Master Huang, but you don't expect them to understand your predicament. They work for your money, not for you."

"And that someone is you?"

I bowed my head.

"So you want to join my organization?"

"With respect, I am only good enough to serve as translator to the best of my ability. With me at your side, you will not be deceived by these crafty devils and will always stay a step ahead. I am otherwise without talent; and am poor in martial arts." I replied. "No I do not wish to be part of Lo Hup Tong." Just to make it crystal clear.

"A secretary then," Old Master Hwang sipped his tea. The silence that followed was deafening. "I could use a secretary," he mused, stroking his beard. I was getting impatient. From my days at Old Master Lee, I know it would take a whole day to conclude a discussion or business transaction even though their minds are made up early on. I shuffled my feet subconsciously. His eyes narrowed at such rudeness. I quickly bowed my head.

"What do you want in return?" Old Hwang asked, after sipping his tea.

"The privilege to learn from you; the chance to fortify our Chinese brethren; a monthly salary and the protection of your name," I replied, pointing at the glaring bodyguard next to him. "Essentially, everything he enjoys."

The old man laughed.

"Well put. You have a way with words, little brother. I am sold. Be sure to report to Old Lam here tomorrow morning. You will get a chance to prove yourself to me very soon."

At this point, he would expect some effusion of gratification and a kowtow.

Time for another gamble.

I took out my hand. He hesitated. I began to count till 5. At the seventh second, he took it and laughed heartily, slapping my back. I hope my hand was still warm at that time. Just then his bodyguard with the face scar whispered something to the old man.

"My man Hung here said you used to work for Old Lee. Didn't he feed you enough?" his eyes narrowed again at the mention of his most bitter rival.

I have been dreading this question and was relieved when it came.

"My father became Old Master Lee's employee before I could even walk. And yes, I grew up on Old Master Lee's rice. But as you know, the Old Master is no longer dragon head. I have no fealty to the new head, or the Sam Hap Tong," I replied truthfully.

Old Hwang stroked his beard again, which I now interpret as a sign of a favorable response.

"Very well, we shall see. Although you are not Lo Hup Tong member, bear in mind that the punishment for betrayal will be the same for you."

I recognized Scarface the moment he stepped into the room. The whole time he never took his eyes off me, snarling like a dog. I swore I even saw saliva dropping off the corners of his mouth.

He was my childhood bogeyman.

When my father was a mere henchman to Old Master Lee, the Lo Hup and Sam Hup tongs were in the middle of a vicious turf war. In one of the melee, my father; shielded the Old Master and slashed the attacker across the face. Ever since, Big Hung had vowed revenge; but the turf war was ended by diplomacy and my father was promoted. Hung was forbidden by his master to lay a hand on my father lest he triggers another war. In the underworld, he was also known as Syphilis Hung; probably due to his insatiable romps in the whorehouses and the fact that he's psychotic; especially in battle; an asset to the paranoid Old Master Hwang. As a child, whenever I disobeyed my father or Old Ma, 'scarfaced syphilis Hung' would get me in the dark of the night. In person, he seemed much smaller than in my imagination. Still, I cursed my luck for running into him so quickly. He needed to be dealt with but first of all I need to prove my worth to Old Master Hwang.

Once sojourner-workers signed their papers with the white companies, Old Hwang absolved all responsibility on the workers. If their families did not pay the remaining fees by the stipulated time, a system of progressively escalating violent reminders would be initiated against them. Complaints amongst the workers were directed at the foreman, who had the unique role of advocate for the workers as well as spokesman for the Tongs. Some sojourners were success stories, especially in the early days of gold mining. When the gold dried up, the railways were not as lucrative for the workers. Some essentially became slaves. But the Golden Mountain perpetually hungered for workers to alter her landscape. And for some reason, men kept coming. And Old Master Hwang became wealthier.

Amongst the dragon heads, Old Master Hwang was the shrewdest. He understood the concept of monopoly. Constantly on the lookout for rivals, and kept abreast with the latest news, it was no wonder his tong was the most popular, a stepping stone for every Chinese youth who aspired to be successful in Chinatown. Every whore aspired to be Old Hwang's next mistress or wife.

For these reasons, I found myself hunkering down a plan in his opulent office on how to maintain his monopoly in the face of considerable opposition; most of which was the Act. We bickered about some details. He would balk at the risks he had to take. I had to concede to put myself on the line; but only with certainty I would have his backing. I maintained a respectful stance as I coddled, threatened and cajoled the old fox. In the end we reached a compromise. We shook hands again. Old Master Hwang grinned in excitement, revealing his gleaming gold tooth. I shuddered every time. Over the next few days, I laid out my plans for Old Master Hwang. He ran a neat operation for bringing workers over from China. He had recruiters in the troubled cities and villages of China who enticed impoverished folks to seek a better fortune in the Golden Mountain. As in the case of my father, the recruiters didn't have to do much. Folks voluntarily flocked to them. Once the fee was agreed upon, and the deposit paid, everything else would be taken care of. There will be guaranteed jobs. Once they started working, they could begin to send money back to their families; through a money-courier service owned by Old Hwang, for a small service fee. Their families could then pay the rest; within a stipulated time. Old Master even owned the ships he used to bring the men over. Ostensibly carrying oriental import produce; all contained a secret hold that could accommodate thirty to forty men in squatting positions.

Once they arrived, they would be chartered by rail or carriage to the multiple different companies that had dealings with Old Master Hwang. All this while, it was mostly a tacit agreement. Money changed hands when the human cargo arrived. Old Master Hwang seek to control the price per head as he saw please. However, the one problem was that the white devils' side of business did not run with equal efficiency. The local railroad and mining companies were not sympathetic to Old Master Hwang's intricate planning effort into maintaining such an extensive and delicate network. No, they were more concerned with getting the cheaper labor while appeasing the increasingly organized local unions and politicians who were feeling uncomfortable with the tireless workers from China. The dragon head in the eyes of the Americans was a wormy crook, an inconvenient but sometimes necessary evil. Because of this variability, Old Hwang occasionally found himself in a glut, too many workers without available jobs; or worse, insufficient workers for a contract, and snapped up by the competition. With my bi-lingualism, I could provide him with information from the San Francisco Gazette and elsewhere to know which company is on which project as well as which local union is agitating against the Chinese. That way, he knew exactly when to jack up his prices and when to lie low. My reading has diminished greatly since university but I still start my day with a quick survey of all the English dailies which I procure from a blind Negro peddler just off Stockton (with Old Hwang's money). In those days I took interest only in matters concerning Chinese immigrants; and they were enough to keep me occupied. To the ignorant bliss of Chinatown's inhabitants, there was mounting hostility towards the presence of Chinamen in California. From the 'sensational' rumor that a Chinaman married a white woman out west to the recent Supreme Court's academic decision over admission of a Chinese child to public school; they all rattled nerves; white nerves. These predictable sentiment fluctuations were extremely profitable to local law enforcement.

Local enforcement was in the form Sergeant Williams; a portly Irish who hated Chinamen but loved their gold. Old

Hwang suspected that he was on the Sam Hup Tong's payroll, as their dens were left untouched whenever a raid was performed. And it would usually ensue following a public outcry or a 'yellow menace' scare. Though I suggested that such hysteria could be predicted fairly accurately by reading the English language papers, Old Hwang insisted on a more secure guarantee. And thus, I found myself one night in urine-stenched alley behind Chinatown Road flanked by two Lo Hup Tong fighting-men. I could hear Sergeant Williams before I saw him, wheezing like an out-of-steam locomotion. A cat leaped out of nowhere and startled me. To my embarrassment, I let out a cry. My companion snickered and patted my shoulder "Don't worry little brother, we have Old Master's orders to keep you safe. If the white devil lays a hand on you, my brother here and I will die with him;" he said assuredly. I was sure he did not think that the vulnerable fat man represents a force much larger than the Lo Hup Tong.

He spat on the ground when he saw us.

He turned to his companion; a taller, less portly white man in priestly garb who was visibly as uncomfortable as me with the surroundings. He had pale skin and wore glasses.

"nee meen yao huo gie"

I did not understand.

He repeated again, with changed inflections. And again. It sounded loosely like 'my mother is a whore' The Lo Hup Tong fighter on my right laughed out loud. Sergeant Williams tugged at his collar uncomfortably, and said impatiently, "Father, tell these chinks we don't have much time and get on with it!"

The white man tried again.

"wo...yao...gen....ni..err....jiao hua...."

I chimed in,

"Excuse me, perhaps I can translate," slowly, in English. Sergeant Williams shot me an irritated look and raised his eyebrows at the priest. "Well, what did he say?"

"I believe he spoke English Sergeant," the anxious priest said.

"Sergeant Williams, Old Master Hwang would like some protection for his business and he is willing to pay," I said. The old priest looked relieved he did not have to translate but alarmed at the conversation that is transpiring.

"How much?" Williams asked simply.

"Old Master is offering twenty-five dollars per week."

"You tell your yellow master to feed that to his dogs," he spat, leering at the high-binders next to me. I paused.

"Old Master understands your hardships and the many constables you have to lead. Thirty five dollars."

"Seventy dollars every week," he sneered, revealing rotten teeth.

"Stop at fifty. I will not help Sam Hap Tong feed their greedy dog," Old Hwang had instructed.

"Tell me boy, how much would your yellow master lose if I decide to just close all his opium dens, whorehouses and drive him and his brood back to his emperor's arse?"

Williams challenged, his eyes narrowed as he studied me up and down, surprised at my English and also excited to see if I would call his bluff.

"But Old Master, the greedy dog is still a vicious dog. And his bite can be very damaging," protested Mister Liu yesterday.

"If it comes to that, our Young Master Lee here will have an interesting role to play," Old Hwang had gestured at me cryptically.

"Old Master Hang had weathered many storms in Chinatown. This will be no different," I said, unsure of the ramifications of my own words.

"Your friends down the street don't think so," he smirked, confirming Sam Ham Tong's patronage. He then moved towards me menacingly. My bodyguards flinched. The fat sergeant, no doubt wishing he had brought his own reinforcements backed away before spitting on the ground, with the frightened priest tittering along.

"Tell your boss that I Peter Williams decides which monkey gets to stay in Chinatown!"

As I walked home, I kept repeating to myself that I am but just a messenger.

MENACE OF CHINAMEN GAMBLING

It was rumored that in the early days, Old Master Hwang's first foray in Chinatown was gambling dens. Nowadays with at least 4 major tongs operational; he still maintained one of the largest underground gambling networks. The ones reserved for high rollers were literally underground; of which only Lo Hup Tong's chief lieutenants have access. He maintained a few above ground dens to serve as sentry post and as decoy for local enforcement.

I had been waiting in the smoke-filled gambling den the whole morning. The gambling tables were held in the same room as an opium den. The air was thick and blue with opium smoke; mixed with the balsamic aroma emanating from multiple joss sticks offered to Guan Yu, the God of Righteousness in the central altar. The fumes floated to the ceiling, finding no vents to escape, drifted heavily down on our heads, suffocating my lungs; completely without trace of the virginal aroma of my experience at the dorm with Chen Ping. There were about 10 tables in all, hosting a variety of pai gau or fan tan. The players were mostly workers of Old Master Hwang, feeling confident they would win more money from their boss on their off days. No matter how many times events proved them wrong; they always felt confident enough for another round. Around the corner in the den were regular patrons, eyes glazed over as they danced with the celestials.

At the head of each table sat the dealer with a bag containing black and white buttons. He would scoop down into the sack with his bowl and raise it, turning it upside down on the table. The players then bet on the combination of the remaining buttons. Flanking the dealer would be well-fed muscular lookouts. Anyone caught cheating or winning too much would be immediately removed to the backroom where severe interrogation would take place. Old Sing, a half blind cripple who served as cleaner of sorts, would often emerge from the backroom holding a grisly human thumb gingerly, humming a country folk song as he did.

I was beginning to feel nauseous and bored when the alarm sounded for a raid, in the fashion of pots and pans clanging in ever increasing ferocity. The first line of lookouts for the den was placed right at south end of Chinatown Road, half a mile away. There was plenty of time to convert the den into an empty hall or anything we wish to. Old Hwang's lieutenants entered the den and ushered all the customers into an adjoining makeshift room, which tunneled into the rice store across the street. There, the patrons would emerge into the street nonchalantly, without a single grain of rice on their hands. A few disgruntled patrons were reluctant and insisted on collecting their winnings. These were promptly shown reason attached to the gleam of a hi-binder's dagger. A full five minutes before the San Francisco Police force entered with pomp and baton wielding, Old Hwang's den consist of but a couple of opium smokers too old to move nor care and about ten of Old Hwang's lieutenants, including me; sitting at a table, sipping tea. The captain cursed and started barking instructions to his goons. Then he started to confer with his 2nd in-command, about the reporters outside, the need to catch Chinamen in the act of gambling under instructions of the mayor, about some mole selling out raid to the chinks, about how the Chief is going to 'skewer' them for this. I understood every word.

Nonetheless we were arrested anyway and were all hauled into the paddy-wagon. While climbing the paddy-wagon, a reporter was on standby outside.

"Hey officer, get this chink to smile for the camera" a cameraman jumped from the wagon.

"Stop there you! The cop pulled the collar of the man behind me.

My fellow captives looked blankly as the flash blinded their eyes momentarily, jumping backwards to catch their fleeing souls. This was construed as an escape attempt and hard truncheon blows landed, breaking at least one leg.

I returned the glazed stares of my fellow Chinamen with one of my own as we rode in the paddy wagon like animals. The station was a dilapidated building with a constant hue of blue hanging over our heads. The sudden sight of so many well-fed, uniformed, Chinamen-hating, menacing white devils with weapons struck a bolt of fear in me. I tried to summon the courage of the Monkey King as he overturned Heaven and clenched my fists to keep them from trembling.

"What's with so many Ching-Chongs, Ralph?"

"Gambling den raid," Ralph said simply with a shrug.

"You guys nabbed chinks from Chinatown?" Ralph's colleague's eyes widened in amazement.

"Yeah, the boss works in mysterious ways," Ralph seemed like one who's more comfortable carrying out orders rather than think about them.

"Well, don't break too many bones now. Don't want em chink sympathizers breathing down our necks."

The chuckle Ralph gave made me want to cry.

"Use-less white devil sons of whores!" The man behind me hissed loudly; evidently did not understand the conversation that just transpired. He was even skinnier than me. I felt the slightest envy for him. Ignorance is the fuel of blind courage.

The worst turned out to be true when all of us were huddled into a cell and the door was locked. It was an inner room in the station with no windows or ventilation. There were about seven of us; but it felt like seventy after a while and the cell turned into an oven. Just when I thought I would pass out from the heat, the door flung open and five policemen bearing heavy truncheons came in. One of them was a woman. They first aimed for Big Ox; whom I acquainted from the hostel. The fear in the room was palpable. When the giant Big Ox fell from a blow to the head, our morale plummeted with him. Some men yelled loudly while most understood the situation and took their beating in stride. When my turn came, I whispered to the cop in clear, precise English:

"I have an urgent message for the Chief Inspector." He hesitated. He might just have given me a beating anyway. That might displease his boss. He called for his underlings to bring me to the Chief. I started to breathe again.

The name at door was James Tucker. Chief Inspector.

The underling cop knocked twice and opened the door; and shoved me into a tobacco smell filled room occupied by a lean white man pouring over some documents at his cluttered desk, a cigarette in his mouth and ashes dropping on his lap.

"Sir, this chink says he has an important message for you,"

Chief Inspector Tucker nodded and waved him away.

He sat staring at me for what seemed like minutes.

"You speakee English, yes?"

"Yes, Chief Inspector, as a matter of fact, I do"

His eyes widened with surprise.

"You're one of them who were born here, aren't you? Who taught you to speak like that?"

Gripping my trousers to hide my sweaty palm, I inhaled deeply to redistribute my qi.

"University of California."

"Really," he was visibly impressed, envious and disbelieving. I pressed on.

"And yes, I was born in America," my nervousness got the better of me as I frantically looked into my coat pocket to produce my birth certificate, while silently cursing myself for leaving it in my tin box under the bed at the hostel.

Fortunately, the inspector dismissed my actions and gestured for me to sit. He held up a box of cigarettes. I allowed myself a sigh of relief.

He was curious about my background.

Why don't I sport a queue – My father tells me I am an American citizen sir, not a subject of the Emperor. – followed by his shaking of head in disbelief.

I speak English so well, why not be in school or something – I have no financial means and no sponsors.

After the usual what-do-you-ask-when-the-Chinaman-could-speak-your-language routine, and my well-guarded responses, he seemed satisfied. He did not know I was rounded up with a gang coolies and I saw no reason to remind him of that.

"Oh and what message did you have for me?"

That took me by surprise, but I was ready.

"It is from Old Master Hwang. As representative of the Chinese sojourners, he wishes to inform you that The Chinese Consul in New York has been notified of the police mistreatment of Chinese workers here and will be coming in the near future for an inspection."

His faced reddened. I didn't think he was involved with the regular harassment of Chinese workers by his goons but he certainly turned a blind eye to it.

"However, The Chinese Consul will first communicate with the Chairman of the Chinese Benevolent Association; of which Master Hwang currently fills the capacity."

"You have some nerve, son; talking to me like that,"

I stiffened.

"I am merely the mouth of Old Master Hwang. Be mindful to not punish the messenger." A tinge of fear crept into my voice.

"Give me one reason why I shouldn't arrest you and old pirate Huang and his lot for human smuggling. I have enough evidence to have him deported to China and never come back," he thundered.

I began to think Old Hwang completely miscalculated his strategy. I had to improvise.

"Sir, I am a translator and am not Lo Hup Tong! I put up my hands to reveal my bare hands. Lo Hup Tong members wore a ring on their last finger on their left hands as a sign of identification. "You may do to Lo Hup Tong what you wish but my only crime here is being bilingual and in perhaps in the eyes of some people; that I am Chinese."

The Chief Inspector's eyes softened.

The American is a study of irony. Chinese sojourners were generally universally resented. Their purported extraordinary capacity for suffering and labor made them somewhat subhuman and definitely unwelcome in American society. The more tolerant viewpoint adamantly refuted such notions but declared that the Chinese people are indeed human beings and should be accorded with rights and dignity as such but their strange customs and unintelligible language made them incompatible with American society. But for those who are here, should be spared and protected by oppression even when brought upon by their own kind. That which is unacceptable for the Irish, Scotsman, English should be likewise for the Chinaman. There have been some very telling articles expounding these views in the local broadsheets. Mostly affecting the negroes, and sometimes chinamen.

The bottom line is; the fewer Chinese in America, the better.

That was what I told the Chief Inspector, in the least patronizing manner I could afford.

"I appeal to your human decency, Chief Inspector; to see that The Chinese Exclusion Act is unjust and tramples on the Chinese people, enacted by a minority to safeguard their own financial interests. We --- the Chinese are a dispossessed people; and angry, now that the government is separating husbands from wives, fathers from children. You have seen how resilient they are in the face of such adversity. With Old Master Hwang gone, there will be other Hwangs that take his place; a hundred others, who will not have a representative here in your office; who will wreck absolute havoc in Chinatown. The Chinese value above all, harmony. Old Master Huang seeks to preserve that harmony. If we can come to an understanding, the importation of Chinese workers and the good work of the police out there can be..." I struggled to find the words... "Harmoniously tailored."

I stopped and held my breath.

It took him a while but he did get the message.

"So what does Hwang want?" he asked slowly.

"Sergeant Williams, sir."

All the Chief Inspector did subsequently was to nod and waved me out. I did not dare insist on a more tangible reply but walked out as calmly as my furiously beating heart allowed me to. My relief did not last very long. As soon as I came out of the station I was huddled by a gang. A gunny sack was put over my head and the last thing I saw was the swirling of a queue before the beating began. The first blow was to my head, which unfortunately did not render me unconscious. I bent over and cover my testicles as the blows rained on my back. At least one assailant identified my head underneath the gunny sack and started raining kicks on it. One made contact with my face and my nose bled profusely. I screamed then kept silent, not knowing which would encourage them to go on. I was beaten even more severely than I would have had in the station. After what seemed like all my bones were broken, they stopped and each of the men spat on me.

This was the kind of man Old Master Hwang was. He would set up his own men and me just to ensure his plots run without a hitch. A true strategist.

"That would teach you to be a traitor you useless son of a whore," my assailants said in Cantonese.

Since that day, my knowledge of English became ever closely guarded than before.

Nonetheless, I began to enjoy a special status in Chinatown. Being seen with both white authorities and Chinese underworld powers may irk some people but to most other folks it was a sign of some undetermined importance.

There were two kinds of Chinese immigrants in Chinatown. One was the educated class and the other the laborers. The former group viewed anything un-Chinese with disdain. Eating with fork and knives were barbaric. The women here are loud, hairy, distasteful, have large feet. The men or 'white devils' have no manners and drink tea that taste like urine. Damn them and this forsaken rock to hell! And they would spend their days in tea houses spinning yarns about their own gilded lives in China. What was always left unsaid was the fall from glory that landed them here in the land of barbarians in the first place. And Chinese gentlemen are too polite to enquire that of each other. They usually kept their queues and dressed immaculately, both inside and outside their houses. They remind me of Chen Ping's description of his father.

The second group also has the same goal; that to get out of this country as quickly as possible. They usually kept to themselves, indulging in the usual gambling and whoring to numb their suffering. Their queues are unkempt; most have even cut them off for practical purposes.

One day as I was walking along the dusty streets of Chinatown, on my way to collect the day's earnings from one of Old Hwang's gambling dens, a chore I detested. The old fox had taken to treating me like Lo Hup Tong lackey. Seething with rage at the duplicitous old man and my own impotency, and amidst the cacophony of the shopkeepers, the brothels and gambling dens, I was distracted by a distinctly educated voice; one ringing with elegant words and rousing tone, one I've always imagined in my mind but never heard before. It was coming from one of the many clan associations which usually serve as nothing more than fronts for triads and extortionists. I peered in through the smoke and saw young man, not much older than me speaking to a dwindling crowd. He was talking about the Old Country, the Central Kingdom, China and the momentous changes she is undergoing. The Revolution is underway, he says. China will soon be a Republic and her people will soon be free of the yoke of the foreigners and incapable rulers. I feel sorry for him. He was losing the crowd. Between eking a living and feeling homesick, the people of Chinatown simply had no stomach for a revolution.

Strangely, the Old Country invoked in my thoughts of my father, and his dying wish. I didn't know how to get about it. I shyly mentioned this to Brother Robinson in my letter to him which spanned three pages, with felicitations, and update of my condition, a detailed description of Old Hwang. I inserted the part of my father's wish in a thick paragraph, half hoping he would not notice it.

Two weeks later, I got his one-line reply:

"Ai-ya just get a mui-po!"

Finding a good mui-po or matchmaker was no easy task. They did not advertise their business openly and relied solely on word-of-mouth. The good ones usually kept a very select clientele. The ones who do not have contacts to rich and connected families were usually cons. It was with no small degree of risk that I engaged one based on third party recommendations. As well, I was reminded that the good ones would never ask for money up front. The one I engaged; known throughout Chinatown as Lan-Yi, did not ask for money up front; but did remind me of her finder's fee should the match is successful. Lan-Yi turned out to be an old hand. Over hot tea at a teahouse, she asked some structured questions about my background and my requirements in a girl. She took no notes and seemed to have committed everything to memory. She told me that she did not

Not have anyone off the top of her mind at that time but promised to keep a lookout for me.

And so my mui po set to work. 'Lee Seong; twenty-two years of age; no living relative; healthy body; one of Old Master Hwang's topmost able assistants, is looking for a bride. Does not need to be very beautiful. Humble background with good moral grounding. And of course, healthy in body and a virgin.' was spread by word of mouth to all wives, and mothers, spinsters, widows, whores, mui-pos in Chinatown and beyond.

It seemed Lan-Yi had a template made ready regardless of what I told her. The very next day Lan-Yi contacted me; there was already a candidate! Eighteen-year-old virgin from the respectable Gu family; somewhat educated

"The parents were very reasonable. They only requested a modest dowry…"

"I need to see her first."

"What?"

I repeated my stance.

"Don't be silly boy, you don't get to see the bride until the wedding night. Since your parents are but saints, Lan-Yi will stand in their stead," she smiled sweetly.

"Absolutely not. It is my wedding, and I must see who I'm marrying."

"My boy, you need to trust Lan Yi in these things. I've matched so many couples in my lifetime…"

"Lan Yi, you are one the best matchmakers, of a quality worthy of the gods. But whoever I'm marrying I need to see her first," I matched her sweet smile with mine.

Her sweet smile was disappearing.

"She is a virgin! Do you think she would acquiesce to see you just because you want to?"

"Without me seeing her first there will be no wedding." I said firmly.

Her expression switched to a menacing snarl.

"You chicken fart useless of a man! If you don't trust Lan-Yi you go find your own damn wife!"

After she left in a huff, I finished my tea and ordered breakfast. Well, at least I exposed a fraud.

I crossed the street and saw a butterfly. I paused to remember what the Tung Sing says about meeting a butterfly in the afternoon. Or must it be meeting a butterfly in one's house? I decided to follow the insect as I mentally calculate my birthday and search for the astrological significance of this peculiar encounter.

In those days, there was never a white person who dared step foot in Chinatown, unless they're heavily armed, or part of a mob. And the butterfly led me right to a corner end of Mission Street where three Caucasian individuals; one man and two women were standing on a street corner handing out pamphlets. It was a windy afternoon and the pamphlets they handed out kept flapping back onto their faces. I was most amused and lost all interest in the butterfly. The crowd on that street was sparse and mostly consisted of busy housewives who were illiterate but accepted the pamphlets readily to use as stove kindling. Yet a common perception was of course every Chinaman would recognize the Chinaman script. The second woman intrigued me. There was something unusual in which the way she ventured out from the trio; in a pretext to hand out a pamphlet, but in reality she just wanted to venture out.

Without even glancing at them, I knew what those pamphlets were about.

The Jesus religion.

The platform of the Western powers.

A hope of divine Love.

The scourge of the Chinese people.

The salvation for all mankind.

They reminded me of Chen Ping and Wen Seng.

A gust of wind blew her pamphlets out of her hand and into my face.

The next second, I knew she was in front of me.

"lei ho ma? Wo men pai kai jiao yao ta gao jung guo ren' We are spreading the good news to the Chinese people," she said earnestly.

I stared blankly. Not for her courageous attempt at the tongue-twisting Cantonese and the very alluring accent she lent to it. Not for the fact she has mixed it with Mandarin. Most white preachers do that. Not her bright blue eyes. From Peach Blossoms and other Caucasian girls I met at the University of California, this one made my heart skip a beat.

And so I remained speechless with my mouth opened. I suddenly became self-conscious of my bruised face from the beating a week ago. She smiled and thrust a pamphlet at me. I took it.

My mouth still would not close.

That night, back at the hostel, I lay awake with my eyes wide open. Most of the 40 men or so in that packed room were asleep on their straw mats, in all manner of cacophony. The snorers plowed through their slumber without a care in the world. The homesick ones wailed out in the middle of the night to their loved ones in China. There were several sleepwalkers who wake up in the morning in unusual and compromising circumstances, much to the mirth of the rest.

Unfortunately for me, the man next to me was known as 'Masturbator Chan'. While other men would keep their sexual urges in private, Masturbator Chan would whip his penis out in the open and noisily jerked it until he ejaculated, spreading his seed up in the air, landing on himself and sometimes on others. He claimed he was completely asleep when we confronted him in the morning. Nobody believed that. I swore to him that if his semen ever touched me, I would strangle him in his sleep. He no longer thought it was funny after that. Nonetheless, I acquired the unusual and non-Chinese habit of sleeping with sheets over me. Always.

The ones with money would sneak off to procure prostitutes. They would spend a significant portion of their savings that way. The ones who didn't usually either: had moral inhibitions, lost their money in gambling, or were extremely quiet about their sexual exploits. There is a fourth group, of which I was the only member, extremely shy and uninformed in these matters.

Once I went with a group of men to solicit for prostitutes, after Masturbator Chan offered to pay half for me, perhaps as compensation for having to tolerate his deplorable nocturnal behavior. Although Old Master Hwang probably controlled the huge stake of the prostitution business in Chinatown, I've never seen him enter one. In fact, he seemed to distance himself from the women when they arrive in his boats. Unlike their male counterparts, women from China usually were in more dire straits. Disowned or sold by their families, the older ones end up as indentured domestic servants. The younger ones would almost certainly be prostitutes if they were not betrothed to a husband here or procured by someone.

Unlike the gambling dens, they were at least clean and orderly. There was a waiting room filled with impatient and dirty looking men, with standing room only. The caretaker was a bald bespectacled old man behind a counter with an abacus, collecting money from the customers. There was another well-built younger man that everyone called Wong Gor or Brother Wong. He was in-charge of assigning turns to the customers and preventing fights. There was no real system to it. Usually, it's a first come first served basis but Brother Wong might allow a VIP to jump queue or kick a troublemaker out. It's all at Brother Wong's discretion.

After waiting for thirty minutes or so, it was our turn. I was nervous. Masturbator Chan hurriedly shoved me into a comely slightly plump woman, probably in her 40s, before scurrying into a room with a younger woman, who called him 'Young Master Chan.'

She was friendly.

'First time?'

I nodded sheepishly.

'Take off your trousers. Or do you want me to do it for you?'

I could not be sure if it was an invitation or threat, but I slid them off obediently. And then she took off her clothes. I marveled at the different intricacies of female apparel. First her cheongsam with its many latches, then a silky underwear. When she turned around, I was dismayed.

I've never seen a naked woman before. Her pendulous breasts were unnaturally large, with grotesquely large round nipples. The skin around it looked rumpled and porous; not unlike freshly plucked chicken in the wet market. And the mound of pleasure that the men like to talk about so much; it looked sweaty and barely visible with the generous amount of fat on her thighs; identified only by the sparse black hair. How could the tight body with well-defined curves like Peach Blossoms degenerate into a lump of unrecognizable masses like that?

She was completely unashamed and glanced at my nakedness with a look of disapproval.

"You may call me Aunt Feng," she said, in a matronly tone not unlike Old Ma's

At that, the very mild erection I was experiencing disappeared like a mouse at the sight of a cat. Aunt Feng looked bemused.

'So, what would you like to do now, young man?'

'Nothing!' I gathered up my pants and ran out of the room helter-skelter. For the rest of the week, I was frightened that I would be impotent for the rest of my life.

That ended my foray with prostitutes.

LITTLE BUTTERFLY FINDS A HOME

Usually at this time, I would be filled with erotic desire and my body will respond in kind. I would fill my thoughts with Peach Blossoms, her curvy hips and ample bosoms and that one time when we were in an illicit embrace, and I had my hands in her blouse before she tore me away.

The next morning after being dismissed by Old Hwang, I headed to a familiar alley for a little fan tan when someone yelled out my name. It was Lan-Yi; all smiles again.

"Young Master Lee! I found just the right girl for you!"

"I need to meet her."

"I know I know, ai-ya!" she cursed, fanning her self as she caught her breath.

"Young virgin, respectable family, just arrived from China, from ZhenZhou village not far from your home village. This afternoon, at the Bamboo Leaf; book a private table and request for partitions around it."

I found myself nervous as I waited for her arrival, yet I was curious. Since the Chinese Exclusion Act, there had been virtually no women arriving on the shores except the ones by Master Hwang's arrangements, who usually end up in his whorehouses.

I was dressed in my best jacket and was wearing a brand new wide brimmed hat.

Lan-Yi promptly showed up with a girl who looked like she was my age; but hard to tell as she was wearing shawl and kept her face towards the floor. She was wearing clothes are didn't quite fit her; a drap cheongsam with a non-matching brooch.

"I'm so hungry," Lan Yi said, just as she sat down. "I need to see what they have in the kitchen" Lan Yi said simply and disappeared, with a wink.

I was suddenly overcome with shyness. I steeled myself by reminding myself I'm carrying out father's dying wish.

"So, your name is Little Butterfly?"

She gave a silent nod. There was an awkward silence.

"Lan Yi tells me you're a virgin." She grew red as a beetroot.

"Well, so am I."

For the first time since we met, she looked up at my face in an expression of surprise.

When she saw my grin, she smiled. The ice was broken, somewhat at an expense.

Little Butterfly was actually a distant niece of Lan-Yi, daughter of her husband's brother in-law. After the third consecutive famine in their little farm in ZhenHai village, several relatives pooled their resources together to buy a seat for Little Butterfly's brother in Old Master's Hwang ship. A day before the slated departure however, her brother disappeared. In view of Old Master Hwang's no refund policy, Little Butterfly volunteered to take her brother's place and promised to return with wealth and success. Her heartbroken parents had no choice.

She cut her hair short and boarded the human cargo ship as a man. When she arrived at the Golden Mountain, she searched for her Lan-Yi whom she calls 'Aunty'.

Little Butterfly had no idea that her aunt was sending to meet a suitor. Lan-Yi told her I was a potential employer looking for a maid to work in my enormous mansion.

Little Butterfly told me her story haltingly, in between sobs.

"Young Master, I have no talents. I can cook, wash, sew and farm. If you would take me, I would do anything."

She began to sob loudly; although I could see she was trying her best to stop. Nonetheless I was beginning to bet uncomfortable. I gave her some money and asked her to meet me in front Old Hwang's mansion the next morning. And I paid Lan-Yi her matchmaking fee.

That night, I flirted with the idea of having Little Butterfly as a wife. At last, my father's soul could at last rest. As well, though plainer Peach Blossoms, Little Butterfly was still an angel compared to Aunt Feng and could very well cure my trepidation of female nakedness. In the dark room, with noises of men sleeping, a burning question kept stealing sleep from me:

'Is she really a virgin?'

"Hey Masturbator Wang."

I kicked him wide awake without remorse.

"Eh what?" he said groggily.

"How do I know if a girl is a virgin?" That woke him up right away.

"Simple. If they bleed...," and on he droned about the intricacies of the female anatomy as though he was describing a divine vision he once had but could no longer remember clearly, using repeating words in a confusing and overlapping way. "...but you know what," he finally ended. "Virginity's overrated."

"Then why do men always want a virgin for a wife?"

A loud snore was the reply.

The next morning, as I was approaching Old Hwang's, I spotted Little Butterfly. She was still wearing her oversized clothes and shawl to cover her short hair and was looking about nervously. Her thin frame struck an image of a fragile twig easily snapped into two by the mildest force. I was suddenly filled with pity and vowed to help her any way I can.

I asked her to wait outside.

"My young secretary, what can I do for you?" Old Master Hwang was always courteous, even to the moment he stabs a knife into you. Rumors had it that he was of considerable learning back in China and even passed the Imperial Examinations. But a court intrigue forced his family out of politics.

"I would like to request Old Master to give my cousin a place over her head." I then told him Little Butterfly's story with some added details.

"She is a very close cousin, and I promised her father I would take good care of her," I added at the end; in case Old Hwang was thinking of one of his whorehouse as 'a place over her head.'

"Well, what do you have in mind?"

"Perhaps you need a domestic maid to maintain this opulent mansion?"

"Splendid. So be it."

A brief discussion with the chief housekeeper sealed the employment. No hard labor. Keep her away from the 3rd Mistress, who just scalded her last maid in a raging frenzy. Wages are determined. On account of my relations, Master Hwang gave a three-month bonus to start off on the side.

Most would attribute the secret to Old Hwang's success to his craftiness, cruelty and his disregard for human life. Few remembered that he was also one of the most generous men in Chinatown; contributing much of the infrastructure that it had before the earthquake. He was the classic Chinese baron enigma.

And so the overjoyed Little Butterfly; after thanking me tearfully and multiple attempts at kowtowing, began life in the Hwang Mansion; saving every single penny to send home; she became at last; a sojourner. I made a point to throw my weight around the housekeeper and the other servants to magnify Little Butterfly's status to avoid bullying.

1952

I opened my Bible and retrieved a postcard from Long Island, New York dated 5th February 1945

Dear Brother Seong

Happy New Year

Hope you are doing well. Chow and I just returned from Hong Kong. He asks that you write to him at once if you need any help with setting up the bookstore. I remember you love English books. I hope you enjoy this one. They assured me that it is the most popular in the stands now.

The children send their love.

Your sister

Siu Tip (Little Butterfly)

As I walked home, I felt like I have achieved a good deed yet felt empty within me. I had no interest in engaging the services of a mui po again. My father's wish remained unfulfilled, and I was still a virgin.

I reached into my pocket and found the pamphlet I received from the fascinating white woman with large blue eyes, brown hair and freckled nose. I tried to overcome myself with shame for longing after a white woman.

One morning I was summoned to the Lo Hup Tong Hall of Allegiance. After getting past the front sentry, I walked along an open corridor that led to a clearing, which converged onto a path from Chinatown Street. Lo Hup

Tong gang members loitered about, casting suspicious glances at me. They all wore their queues around their heads, creating a nationwide identity for themselves as the fearsome high-binders. After a thorough body search by the sentry, I was instructed to wait. Soon Old Hwang walked out from a hidden chamber with his usual retinue of followers. He made a bee line for me and motioned that I get into a sedan chair with him. He wore an angry expression, which unmasked his cruel features. In the sedan, Old Hwang's lieutenant, who always dressed impeccably as a gentleman I know only as Mister Liu briefed me:

"There's a shipment at the pier," meaning human cargo. Mister Liu said in heavily accented Cantonese. His background is Hakka, who themselves were historically sojourners in southern China.

"It is being held at the pier by the yang ren," he said, using the polite term 'foreign people' rather than the ubiquitous 'white devils. Aside from his heavy accent, Mister Liu had a deceptively soft-spoken voice for his high rank in the most ruthless triad gang in Chinatown. I strained to catch his words amidst the bumpy ride and cacophony outside.

"We want you to negotiate directly with the yang ren to get the cargo released. If you succeed, Old Master will see to it that you will be handsomely rewarded." Silence followed.

My heart was thumping out of my chest. Mister Liu, noticing my slacked jaw and cold perspiration, laughed.

"Don't worry little brother. If you fail, there is no punishment. We will just have to snatch the cargo. Many of our brothers' lives will be lost. I have recommended that you are to be our one and only resort to avoid a confrontation." He spoke the words 'don't' fail me' through his bespectacled eyes. Mister Liu nodded towards the opening of the sedan. I glanced and saw hi-binders on every rooftop. On the streets, they were innocuous amongst the populace, recognizable only by their queue wrapped like a turban around their heads and the bulge on their left flanks, which is a concealed hatchet. One of them caught my gaze and smiled, or sneered, I wasn't sure. A chill shivered down my spine. We were surrounded by the whole army of Lo Hup Tong!

The old fox of Chinatown was prepared to wage war on San Francisco law enforcement.

The salty air reached indicated that we have arrived at the pier and the three of us alighted. The pregnant mound of Angel Island was in the distance. I took the time to savor the air and scenery outside of Chinatown. The salty breeze soured immediately upon me spotting hi binders behind every tree, rock and building. The midday sun was scorching. The atmosphere was heavy with dew and stench of impending bloodshed.

"Little brother, this is when you prove your worth to me," said Old Hwang grimly.

Surprisingly, even in the heat of the tension, out of the corner of my eye I kept a lookout for the brown-haired girl. She was not to be found. A group of forty to fifty Chinese men and women were squatting on the ground, surrounded by police in uniforms and carrying truncheons. They were in all manners of destitute and malnourishment. Was that how my father looked like when he first arrived? The pathetic barge they journeyed in was anchored at the pier.

The port inspector was Thomas O'Hara; a fat mustachioed man who spoke with a thick Irish accent and looked like Sergeant Williams' twin brother. He stood waiting for us with a smug smile, flanked by two similarly uniformed lackeys. At his feet squatting was a Chinese man with a huge gash on his head which was profusely bleeding. Stains of his blood were all over O'Hara's truncheon. The poor wretch looked like he was about to pass out. When he saw us, his gaze was one of pleading and gratitude. I tried not to meet his eyes. Old Master Hwang didn't even pretend to notice him. Chief Inspector Tucker warned me if I ever run into O'Hara I would be on my own. Not because he was incorruptible, but his hatred for the Chinese was personal. When his father was laid off the mines due to the abundance of cheaper Chinese labor, he abandoned his family and O'Hara's mother drank herself to death. He became a cop just so he can exact revenge on the hated Chinamen. I felt nauseous and had to steel myself by clenching my fists.

When he saw us approaching, O'Hara spat on the ground. I tried not to look at his bloody truncheon. He said something to his colleagues, and they all laughed uproariously. This man was completely oblivious that he was within striking distance from at least five high-binders hidden from plain view; whose goal in life was to impress Old Master Hwang with an act of courage.

I calculated my steps carefully, not walking ahead of Old Hwang as to make him lose face nor walk too far behind as to appear cowardly. I reminded myself that I, Lee Seong, was here as a neutral party to provide interpretation. Sadly, neither O'Hara nor Old Hwang would see it that way.

Old Hwang, one of the most powerful men in Chinatown walked right up to face off against O'Hara, what to him, a lowly constable.

"This one is such an ugly piece of whore shit," he uttered in clipped Mandarin.

O'Hara bristled and straightened his back and stared right at what seemed to him an inferior species.

"Fuckin chink," he spat. His companions' grip on their truncheons tightened. Out of the corner of my eye, I noticed Mister Liu's subtle movements with his fan. Out of view, all high binders moved into position.

"Good morning officer O'Hara", I greeted him in my calmest voice and flashed my most pleasant smile.

"Eh?"

"Good morning officer," I repeated.

"Eh, say what?"

"Goodee moning sair! Old Master Hwang here to talkee about the peepel"

He grunted. "Well, well, this one could actually speak." He grinned smugly, revealing tobacco stained teeth.

"Sair, can you pleasee let my famil-ees go sair?"

"No way, em chinks didn't have no papers. We are deporting them,"

"But sair, we have papers, see. And master, Master Hwang will pay for papers...say watee...process fees now."

O'Hara snorted in contempt.

"You bribe me you dirty chink, you die," he said raising his stick threateningly. I panicked. O'Hara was obviously waiting for us to bribe him. This posturing confused me momentarily. These 'foreigners' are like unpredictable animals, according to Old Hwang.

I glanced at Mister Liu's expressionless face. He was turning his fan towards the ground. My mind raced.

"Wait! You break my bones Sergeant O'Hara, Mr. Silver will know that the local enforcement is solely responsible for the delay of his important construction project," I blurted quickly.

He could suddenly understand my English. The word 'Silver' seemed to put things into perspective for him. Turnbull Silver was owner of Union Pacific, the largest employer in San Francisco for immigrant labor and often appeared on the headlines of the San Francisco Herald. He was featured often in the broadsheets with the mayor, police commissioner and other bigwigs. And I hoped that now he knew that I know his name would add on to the weight of his next decision.

It did. He put his truncheon back into the holster. Then with surprising speed, he slapped me across the face. The grease of hands left an odorous mark across my cheek. To my horror and shame, tears streaked out of my eyes. I was incensed and hatred enveloped me.

Behind me, I felt Old Hwang took a few steps back. From the corner of my eye, I saw Syphilis Hung rushing towards the unsuspecting nearest policeman. At that split moment of reeling from the humiliation, I had hoped that Syphilis Hung in his mania would take down some of these white devils, disembowel the fat O'Hara and then get killed by the white cops himself the next day. My mind immediately took on the next scenario, where hundreds and thousands of Chinese bodies lying dead on Chinatown streets, drawing childhood memories of how the dead white men's souls needed to be appeased.

"Stop!" I shouted, in English although I had meant it for Old Hwang and Mister Liu. I was loud enough to stop Syphilis Hung in his steps and slink back into the shadows. O'Hara was taken aback; his blue eyes gleamed with pure hatred with a glint of bemusement.

"Yer blackmail me, yer chink?" O'Hara said smugly. "Yer think old man Silver cares for coupla of Chinatown dogs like you?"

"No, he doesn't," I regained my composure. "But he does his railroad. His assistant Mr. Jarvis just procured the new laborers from Old Master Hwang this morning, with the expectation that work on the road is uninterrupted."

It was partly true. Mr. Jarvis does exist but I only read of him in the newspapers. No one from Silver's company directly deals with Chinatown dragon heads. It was all done between middle men. But O'Hara called my bluff.

He pretended to confer with the other cops, and turned to face Old Master Hwang.

"Five dollars every head"

Old Hwang turned to me without flinching once.

"Se be it," he said in Cantonese.

"Masta say yessie" switching back to my pidgin. O'Hara's pudgy face became the color of beetroot.

"Stinkin chinks," he muttered, turning his back to us, his way of a closing the deal.

I looked at Old Hwang. This time his black eyes burnt with pure hatred at that slight. Nonetheless he turned to Mister Liu and nodded ever so slightly.

Mister Liu turned his fan up to its prior position, and began fanning himself calmly. Behind him, a henchman brought out a suitcase that contained the money.

I began to breathe.

Unfortunately, I inadvertently caught a glance at the Chinese men and women skulking on the ground; wearing tattered clothes and anguished expressions; their soulless eyes bearing a mild glimmer of hope at the sight of me. I felt a sudden unpleasant burden upon me. I tried to wipe out that scene from my mind.

Later Mister Liu explained to me in his matter-of-fact demeanor that the Lo Hup Tong was divided into twelve teams of two men each and allocated a cop for each team. Every single cop would've been remorselessly killed that day.

As promised, I ensured that Old Hwang continued to head the largest snakehead organization in town; smuggling Chinese labor for at least 4 large conglomerates in California right under the nose of the Chinese Exclusion Act. These people would work for Union Pacific. Sometimes the cargo would be women, for the men.

O'Hara and his goons then walked off, cursing out loud 'the chinks and their stinking money' 'worthless animals' and so forth. Seemingly out of nowhere Old Hwang's foremen appeared and began to usher the human cargo to their designated waiting area. Things moved with lightning efficiency. The hi-binder assassins never emerged from the shadows. I subconsciously touched my crotch to make sure I did not wet myself. Old Hwang turned to me approvingly.

"You have done well, little brother" he smiled, showing his gleaming gold tooth. Before I could think of something to say to dissociate myself as Lo Hup Tong member, the old man's attention shifted. Form amongst the human cargo, his lieutenants picked out a young girl no more than sixteen years of age.

Then it dawned upon me that the Old Fox of Chinatown almost razed Chinatown to the ground senselessly for a concubine!

I was seething with fear and rage as I walked away from the pier. My mind was reeling with violent thoughts that I walked right into a pole recently erected for electricity. The impact was so hard I was knocked right onto the ground. I heard some guffaws and snickering from witnesses in the vicinity. I have inadvertently ventured out onto where Allen St is today.

In my dizziness and embarrassment, I thought I had indeed lost consciousness and was dreaming, for her face shone on me. Her, the girl with the brown hair.

"Hello," I was breathless and feeling foolish. She smiled.

"What does he want, Susan?" an unattractive voice belonging to an older woman next to her demanded, covering her nose and mouth with her fan. I picked myself up and dusted off. I wish I had flattened my clothes from the night before. I couldn't take my eyes off hers; the like of which belie an intelligence. Such foreign features... yet so familiar.

Ignoring her companions, I ventured forward, noticing their backing off at the sight of the dreaded Chinaman.

"Miss, I believe we met yesterday, I read the pamphlet you gave me and I'm profoundly interested in its message."

I marveled at my fluency. This was the very first time I did not use pidgin to a white woman. In truth, I never read the pamphlet. The mere touch of it triggered a host of confusing thoughts and feelings. Her eyes shone in amazement and appreciation, which warmed the deepest caverns of my heart.

"Really?"

"Indeed, though there are some interesting parts perhaps you could explain to me in detail..." Out of the corner of my eye I could see her two friends staring at me with jaws open.

"Why, that's marvelous. We simply must introduce you to Reverend Woods. He can guide you better than I. The Sinner's Prayer..."

I frowned. I had no desire to meet this Reverend Woods. I searched my mind frantically. Unwelcomed thoughts of Wen Seng reminded me of the sole intentions of these religious zealots.

"I am a little skeptical about certain contents in the pamphlet."

"Rev. Woods is a Scripture scholar. He can explain to you with more clarity."

"Well, I'm not sure if white man will want to talk to a Chinaman."

"Oh, don't be silly, Reverend Woods converts many early converts like you. A Chinaman is as good as any other God's creatures," her smile etched her dimples.

"But..." I struggled to keep the desperation out of my voice.

"You will go to see Reverend Woods, won't you?" she asked earnestly. I have found my upper hand.

I put on my most skeptical face, raising my eyebrow as I studied the pamphlet once more. This fascinating girl is a Christian. If she belongs to the same sect as Wen Seng, this is the moment she could save my soul from the clutches of Hell. I counted to three in silence and smiled in my heart when she said,

"Oh, very well, meet me at the Mission tomorrow and we'll go together. My name is Susan by the way. What's yours?"

"Seong...Lee Seong." Her companions giggled foolishly at the unfamiliar noun.

"That's a nice name, Lee Seong. I'll see you tomorrow at noon."

Seemingly out of nowhere she produced a pen and I held out my palm, wishing it looked cleaner. Susan, without a moment's hesitation held it still and wrote on it; the address of The San Francisco Bible Mission and her name in Chinese; Snow Mountain.

S's

1879 February 5th

At last! Thank the Lord for His Providence and Blessings. Mother and her worries never cease. Chinatown did not seem to be 'borderland of hell'; and the people of China are so delightfully fascinating. The men wear long hair and wear brazenly loose shirts and such quaint shoes! I confess I was discreetly on the lookout for women with small feet but could not see any. Reverend Wood said they have realized it was to their own reasonable reputation to hide their atrocious practice indoors all the time. Sarah was always so eager to convert a heathen but that mousey girl could never open her mouth to anyone but her darling Peter. Besides, her command of the Chinese language is absolutely appalling. Cantonese is a difficult tongue but I am seeing myself making progress. About five words a day, one hundred fifty words a month. I could even construct sentences, which Rev Wren said was flawless! The heat was searing today and I was about to persuade Peter to end our little outing when the most curious incident occurred. It was that Chinese boy from the other day. His aquiline features were shaped into a frown and he wore the same outfit which seemed too old and large on him. He was wearing a cap and I longed to see the curious shaved head but imagine a tuft of fine pitch-black air, straight as a woman's on it. He was walking straight on, no doubt contemplating some Chinamen secret.. I nudged Sarah, and waved at him. The poor little mouse literally hid behind me at the sight of a Chinese man.! Evangelize indeed! And then the funny boy walked right into a pole. How painful it must have been. And he looked so worried. I could not take my eyes off the painful bump on his head, which was quite comical. I must've let out my mirth. May the Lord forgives the sin in us that made us gleeful in another's misfortune. He seemed so disinterested in his head bump. Then he spoke and my heart missed a beat. He spoke English like an American! Hearing English from a Chinese face is so… unusual. And his eyes! So deep and sad I wished I could touch him. Such thoughts! It is true as Rev Wood said. The Chinese are particularly susceptible to the Word of God. I must remember that a heathen is still a heathen, English speaking or not. Hopefully, he will be my first convert. That will show Mother.

Bible Mission

Rivera St

The Bible Mission was housed on the corner of Rivera St where Chinese influence was scant. I arrived with Wen Seng's Bible. I've read certain pages here and there. Seemed to me like a mish mashed compilation of different authors with no central theme. There were some deep philosophical thoughts and some rules on conduct and morality. When Wen Seng tried to point out certain verses to me, Chen Ping and I were too busy ridiculing him to pay attention. Now, in order to impress Susan I wish I did.

Christians were very devoted to the Bible; not unlike Confucians to the teachings the Kung Tze. And there were so many different schools of thought leading to different tribes until no one really knew which the original was. But unlike Kung Tze, Christians claimed a personal interaction with their God, more like a Friend. None of the Chinese Gods could be considered friendly; much less a friend by a mortal and I could see why Christianity flourished so.

I gleaned from Susan's pamphlet that she was from the Baptist tribe.

She was already waiting for me; dressed in a black dress and cap, like a boy; which covered her flowing brown hair.

"Hello," she greeted me.

"How do you do?" I didn't know why my heart started to pound at this point.

"I have something to tell you. I am thinking since you approached me I should be the one who evange..i mean, answer your questions. We could do it in the Mission's library. Would you like that?"

It was exactly what I asked the Jesus God for last night.

We sat in opposite each other in the dank room, poor illuminated and smell of rotting paper and dead cockroaches. An elderly white man manned the entrance, reading a newspaper.

It seemed Susan just started learning Mandarin, from a missionary who just came home from China. He left yesterday, she told me sadly.

"Why did you want to learn Mandarin?"

"To be honest, I don't have any noble aspirations. It's just because I was curious and thought I would be neat to be able to converse in a completely different tongue."

Her straightforward frankness impressed me.

And she sat down to explain the tenets of the Christian faith to me. I summoned all my energy to project an impression of earnest interest.

In my mind, Chinese Christians were represented by Wen Seng; timid, fanatical and if Chen Ping were to be believed, sold out the country to wicked greedy white men who used this religion just as they used their guns and ship; as a tool.

Thankfully, the way her lips moved, her eyes danced, and the shades of her dimpled cheeks change color encouraged me.

"Now shall we say the sinner's prayer together?" she asked.

It sounded like that would signal the end of our meeting.

"I am really sorry," I put on my most contrite face. "I would like to; but it sounded like an enormous commitment. It is hard you know, for one of a different culture to shed his stripes so readily."

"That's alright. Conversion should never be hasty." I detected a tinge of disappointment.

"But," I added quickly. "You have explained the message so well I felt moved. I would like to know the Christian God more. Perhaps we could meet some more to discuss this. Tonight, I will have to counsel with my ancestors and the Chinese gods with this newly acquired information."

"Oh?" her blue eyes danced with curiosity. "What are the Chinese gods like?"

And I went on to describe the various pantheon of gods that I received from both Old Ma and my father. I was delighted at her rapt attention, and incessant questions. Our delightful tête-à-tête lasted till sunset.

"So, Susan, do you think we could meet again?"

She thought for a while.

"Why not? Perhaps at the same time you could help me with my Cantonese, if you don't mind."

"I'll be happy to."

We spent the whole afternoon together. It felt like five minutes.

It was a good day.

MR. THEODORE BUZZ

I finally summed up enough courage to tell Old Master Hwang I no longer wished to run Lo Hup Tong's errands for him. I was strictly, a secretary. The old man's face became expressionless and seemed like he was about to order a beating. Luckily his rational mind prevailed. Now that I've proven my value he could not afford to lose me. His expression changed into a forceful smile and dismissed me with a small 'very well.' As I walked away, I swore I heard the rattling of the tea cup held by Old Hwang's trembling hands in rhythm with my own thumping heart.

I have more free time now. Old Hwang's eldest son returned to China to procure a bride but was turned away from the port when he tried to return to America. The Chinese Exclusion Act was cited. Nothing the Old Master could budge the authorities. His son was born here in San Francisco, but was delivered by a midwife and the old man never bothered to register his birth; not foreseeing that he himself would stay here that long.

The Young Master was being held at the port. I found him squatting on the floor along with a hundred or so passengers from his ship. It began to rain. I walked right up to the nearest guard.

"Excuse me, I need to speak with the port inspector," I hollered over the downpour.

He backed away when he saw me approached; for I was drenched and he was cheerfully dry under the shelter. Before answering, he pushed me out of the post and into the rain.

"Get back Chinaman!" he barked.

"I said, I need to speak with the Port Inspector," I repeated calmly. The familiarity of his tongue dawned upon him. A curious but stern glance ensured I stayed outside in the rain while he fetched his superior officer. An older man in a similar uniform emerged from the office. He had a kind, grandfatherly appearance and immediately invited me into the shelter. He hesitated before shaking my hand as I introduced myself as Mr. Hwang's secretary. I explained to him the situation; that Mr. Hwang's son was indeed born in America before the Act came in place. I handed over to him my letter detailing my presentation, complete with family tree and all. I had taken special pride in my handwritten document. It broadcasted my penmanship, mastery of English and university education. The port inspector took one glance at the letter and before my horrified eyes, tore it to pieces.

"Look Chinaman," his kindly eyes took on a sinister glare. "I don't know and I don't care who you are and where you are form. The law says every chinaman needs to have documentation for reentry. And every one of em chinks over there do not have it."

"But- " I began to protest, foolishly.

"Are you telling me how to do my job?" he asked menacingly. His other lieutenants moved towards me and grabbed me from the back. I was pulled the office. I struggled and spat. My saliva ended on my assailant's face. He retaliated with a punch to the stomach, which downed me and the kicking began. It was the longest beating I've ever had. The wind was knocked out of my stomach I thought I would die. I just hoped I would die un-mutilated so I could come back as a ghost and haunt my murderers. Unfortunately, I was still conscious when they were done. I was dragged out on the enclosure and thrown in with the rest of new arrivals. My precious letter was stuffed into my mouth. I moved all arms and legs, relieved to find none was broken. I lay on the ground waiting for the drizzling rain to wash my open wounds.

"What did you say to them?" the stranger squatting next to me inquired. I was in too much pain for conversation.

"You can speak their gibberish?" he asked again in amazement.

"I'm looking for a Young Master Hwang," I mustered

"Sorry brother. I am not able to help you," he said quickly, his curiosity evaporated at the name Hwang.

I looked around. Strange faces stared back at me. I was taken aback by the emptiness in them. Most of them were staring at the ground, apathetic and wretched and repulsive. Even the abhorrent opium dens of Master Hwang seemed more inviting than here. The familiar, irrational rage against Wen Seng brewed in my stomach. That gave me a spurt of energy as I sprinted across the boulevard and into the streets of Chinatown. When I looked back, no one was in pursuit.

That day was a lesson in hubris I never forgot; a reminder to use English cautiously. Also, that I am a Chinaman.

I reported to Old Hwang my failure. He took it in stride. Then I convinced Old Hwang to procure a gadget known as the telephone after demonstrating to him the nifty device. The old man balked at first; but relented. He had a pylon set up and lines connected to the front of his house. I spent hours a day on learning to navigate the telephony system. It allowed me to call up newspaper offices, lawyers, masquerading as anyone I like.

"Hello, I would like to speak with Mr. Quimby please," getting through after waiting for half hour.

"Who is this calling?" a matronly male voice asked rudely.

"My name is Theodore Buzz, I'm an editor with The Herald. I have an extremely urgent message for him with regards to some revelations regarding his secretary," I said pleasantly.

"What sort of revelations?" a worried tone.

"I'm sorry sir. It is for Mr. Quimby's ears only. Perhaps you can ask him after I relayed to him."

"Hold on."

I tapped my fingers on the panel.

"Quimby here," an important sounding voice.

"Teddy Buzz from The Herald. I am following on a story about the petition you filed for twenty Chinamen at detained at Angel Island. What is the current status of the case and hypothetically, if there is a Chinaman who was born here but does not have documentation proving thus. What are his chances of winning in court?" I spoke quickly in case the line was cut.

"We are still testing the act," lawyer Quimby spoke with the slow flow of a professor. "In your hypothetical case, it is without hope unless you can prove to the judge that the birth took place here."

"Very well, thank you for your comments, Mr. Quimby."

Old Master Hwang then enquired how he might be able to forge an American birth certificate. Not my specialty. But what Old Master Hwang wanted; he got. Three months later, I was introduced to a bespectacled diminutive young man who wore a European style bowler hat and a line of carefully trimmed moustache from Hong Kong by the name of Sebastian Chow; expert forger.

From Susan I learned a lot about how white men lived.

Her father was Corporal Hugh Milton and hailed from a place called Virginia. He was a scion of a wealthy family but died in battle when she was very young, leaving her widowed mother a substantial inheritance from his family business. Rose Henrietta Milton was one of five daughters to teaching couple. Her parents taught at the prestigious Mount Holyoke College. All their daughters completed high school level education; three of whom became teachers and lecturers. In her final year at school, she was swept away by the strapping corporal at a ballroom. Though impressed by the young man, her deeply political parents were apprehensive about the Confederate leanings of the Miltons. Against her parents' wishes, she left damp Massachusetts for dry Virginia. Her influential, wealthy, slave-owning in-laws were equally suspicious of the girl from the north that their son brought home. The fact that her family was landless didn't help her cause. Just then the war broke out. After the honeymoon weekend, Corporal Milton was conscripted and nothing was heard of him for three long months. The long-suffering Rose stayed on in a small cottage just outside Richmond, despite pleadings from her parents to return home. Going home would admit defeat. Besides, she realized she was pregnant. Susan was born in that cottage with the help of a midwife. Unlike most babies she didn't utter a single cry. The worried midwife stayed on to help with nursing. But Susan remained mute. Then inexplicable two months later, the baby girl cried her lungs out. The next day, a letter arrived from the battalion commander informing them Corporal Hugh James Milton died valiantly in battle.

Susan never found out the reason why her mother moved to California; but it was likely from a falling out with her in-laws; as Susan never saw or heard about her father's extended family.

Fortified by her will of steel and her scholarship heritage; Susan's mother Rose set about living the dignified life of a Christian widow carrying her married name 'Milton'; amongst the many war widows. Her two passions in life were church and children.

Susan told me much later, her mother was not so much Scriptural than church-y. The First Baptist was a teeming group of people from dissimilar backgrounds; mostly new arrivals from the East with different flavors, theology, and social interests. Their last names sound fresh and familiarity rarely extended beyond the current generation. It was a place where one could socialize and exert authority on a level playing field.

Susan was never showered with the disproportionate attention or outrageous discipline that sometimes an only child gets. There were always other children her mother surrounded herself with. However, Rose never yearned for any more of her own because she loses interest in them once they reach teenage years when their adorable naïveté gives way to a rebellious curiosity. As a result Susan had many siblings who never grew up.

S's

Since the night when he held my waist and kissed me, I have been hating myself for pushing him away. Worse, why did I have to slap him? Roger Stewart is a despicable creature; a vile beast without the slightest human decency. I have been reliably informed and witnessed myself his debauchery. There is even a rumor he was seen at Mrs. Kessler's when her poor husband was away on business. Yet his mischievous smile! Oh that smile with that contemptible leer!

Thoughts of him still send shivers down my body.

Enough! Oh what have I done!

At least my distraction comes from Seong; my very own intriguing Chinaman who proved to be most fascinating. To think that he even went to University! If he was in China, he would be an official or a distinguished gentleman. When he spoke, his speech was deliberate, almost as if translating from Chinese first, yet his diction is perfect. He is always exceedingly, sometimes annoyingly polite. He never asked a question about me although I could sense he wanted to. He reminds me of a tranquil Chinese garden surrounded by an impenetrable invisible wall which I, an outsider could only peer from outside I wish I could tear down those invisible walls and peer into his mind.

I sometimes let on to Mother than I have been seen in the streets of Chinatown with a Chinaman. Her icy response belies a fury that satisfies me. I do notice that he was attracted to me, my delightful Seong. Although it was an impossible situation, I am starting to compare him in every respect with that insufferable cad Roger Stewart. A pity the Chinese are so aloof with their emotions.

There were many suitors from the church in which she was very active but she rejected all in her stern matronly manner, claiming privately that Californian men were rough and 'unrefined'.

The constant worry Rose had was the lack of a father figure for Susan; especially as she noticed her daughter beginning to blossom as a woman and attracting boys' to the house; so much so she even considered the proposal of old deacon Watts for Susan's sake. To her relief, Susan took to religion which afforded a level of protection and conservatism Rose herself could not provide.

Left with only his memory, Rose's Hugh was the most perfect man who ever lived; his imperfections faded to the land of forgotten memories never be brought again by the living embodiment. In the early days in California, Rose's one guiding compass when faced with a difficulty would be 'What would Hugh do?"

To Susan, her mother was like a best friend, favorite aunt and sometimes strict headmistress all rolled into one, in a no less confusing order. Like most mothers, (or fathers for that matter) they want to see their daughters live their unfulfilled lives. She yearned for Susan to be an educated, independent woman like a Bostonian. The highest level of education that California has for most girls ended at thirteen; with emphasis on basic reading and taking care of the home. The very few I saw at the University of California were from privileged families.

When to her delight Susan professed a love for books and proved to be an able scholar, Rose ensured that reading materials were never short in the house. 'Men's books' were procured or borrowed.

At a young age, Susan was fascinated by missionaries and their tales of lands faraway. Unlike other girls, she took her fascination one step further; in wanting to become one. She experienced her first spiritual awakening at the age of fourteen, when she upon hearing she was felt a burden for the unsaved, lost souls of the world.

The words of Isaiah 53:7 resonated in her very soul:

"How beautiful upon the mountains are the feet of him who brings good tidings, who publishes peace, who brings good tidings of good, who publishes salvation, who says to Zion, "Your God reigns."

I hesitated for a moment before accepting Susan's invitation to church. I have been to church services while in university; it was like sitting through a long lecture. When I used to accompany Old Ma to the temple, she would just supplicate her needs and wants, burn some incense, donate some money to the monks and we're off. I didn't mind church services at that time. But now I was apprehensive about how her folks might think of Susan for bringing a Chinaman into their sanctuary. Misunderstanding my hesitancy, she assured me that the First Baptist was a vibrant open family led by the all-wise Reverend Woods who has a deep passion for the souls of the Chinese people.

Hesitant or not, I knew I would go; because then I could see Susan even on a Sunday.

My favorite part of the service was the singing. There I could sing in English at the top of my voice. It was a liberating feeling. My least favorite part was the much admired Rev Woods – a man who's the very embodiment of the 'evil white man' in Chinatown A tall, red-faced man with prominent sideburns and a balding spot, he reminded me of the aloof professors in university; hiding their hatred behind a façade of education. There's something else about Nathaniel Woods that did not sit well with me; other than the fact my sweet Susan kept gushing about him. His deep eyes that were described as intelligent seemed cunning to me. His much admired baritone voice of confidence belies a violent proclivity to me.

At the end of the service he would pray aloud:

"Oh God Almighty we beseech Thee to lay a burden upon our hearts to reach out to the Chinee; so the light of Christ might shine into their dark lives! Open their eyes that they might abandon their idolatry, slavery and violence that are an abomination unto Thou. One day this great country will Thou protect thy people whose lives are in danger there while spreading Thy Holy Word and civilization upon all four corners of the heathen land. Amen!"

After service, His Pomposity would come to shake my hand.

"Sair! How you!"

"O me veli good!"

"Son, have you accepted the Lord Jesus into your heart, and ask that He forgives yours sins, and renounce your gods?"

"Yesy- yesy. Jesus my god now. All other gods rubbish!"

"That's very good young man. Tell your fellow countrymen about the Good News"

"Gud news, Veli guuudee!

I would so love to punch this man in the face.

Later, as we were walking home, "Why do you mock Rev Woods like that? Susan asked reproachfully.

Hurt by the question, "I didn't" I denied.

"Yes you did. You use pidgin on people you don't like. Don't think I never noticed."

It was true.

"I just don't trust him." I said sourly and tried to change the subject.

I did promise that for her sake I would not make fun of the Reverend Woods again.

In my joy and gallivanting, I never could forget the slap, from the greasy hands of one that is not my parents. A hateful rather than an instructional gesture; designed to humiliate. The ringing echo across the pier, the public humiliation stuck with me. Whenever the memory gripped me either in my daytime reverie, or nighttime sleep, I would become extremely restless and every fiber of my body screamed for revenge. How does a Chinaman get back at a white policeman?

"Hello, San Francisco police station."

"Harlow, I want makee report on badee fan tan gambling in arr..Chinatown Street ah next to de post office..." I finally got through after spending 10 minutes with the operator.

"Hold a minute there. How did a Chinaman get hold of a telephone?"

I hung up and cursed myself. I waited a whole hour and tried again. Twenty minutes later,

"Hello, this is Theodore Buzz from The Herald. We are following up on reports that the San Francisco police has failed to act on several gambling dens –"

"Hold on"- followed by the sound of distant paper shuffling.

"Detective Hamilton speaking."

I repeated my introduction.

"We haven't got any reports of that--"

"Maybe you haven't but police inaction over on Montgomery Street has riled some feathers. Look detective, this is strictly hush-hush. But I have on good evidence that Sergeant O'Hara is on the take with the chinks." I hung up.

I wasn't sure if it would work, but I did begin to sleep better after that.

I chose my alter ego because the words 'Theo' and 'Buzz' were most difficult for the Chinese tongue, and thus would rouse the least suspicion.

Old Master and I did visit Lawyer Quimby at his office. He did not recognize the Theodore Buzz from The Post. A wizened man who looked as professorial as he sounded, he listened to our situation patiently but reiterated his stand on the futility of it all. But Hwang's gold did persuade Quimby to put his son's name on his habeas corpus petition anyway.

Old Hwang spat in front of Quimby's office as we left. Instead of the trishaw, he elected to walk home and signaled me to follow him. I hated to be seen walking alongside the dragon head in Chinatown. People instinctively leave us a wide berth, knowing there were probably invisible high-binders ready to strike at any perceived threat towards the Old Master. Some cast me admiring glances, that I should be so close with the most successful man in Chinatown. I felt I could accept that compliment, as long as I was not perceived to be Lo Hup Tong.

"Little brother you have done a lot of good work for me. I pay you yes, but I know a sincere man when I see one. I have a gift for you," the old fox began, as though I was his son. He stopped speaking. We turned a sharp corner into a back alleyway, I remember from when as a child I would come with Fat Chen to watch a couple of stray dogs mate. Fat Chen would throw stones intermittently at the mating animals, to constantly interrupt the mounting. I remember marveling at the tenacity and stupidity of the animals, to keep doing it in spite of the danger and threat.

There were no animals in heat today for there were a couple of Lo Hup Tong members standing guard. Behind them was a bloody pulp that resembled a naked man. The red tuft of hair was all that could be recognized as Sergeant O'Hara. There were either body parts lying elsewhere on the ground. Standing astride the body was Syphilis Hung; and caught his cold, methodical eyes which acknowledged the presence of his master. He was holding a bloody machete.

"Hung, make sure his body is not found anywhere near Chinatown," Old Hwang warned. Then he threw me a self-satisfied glance and walked away.

I walked away from the area in a direction opposite from it all, my heart feeling heavier than when it was bogged down by the lust for revenge.

One palpable change in Chinatown compared to when I was growing up was its shrinking size. The sojourners have always been my community. For those who were born here, we never really believed that one day all Chinamen will return to China. I heard the Lee Clan was influential somewhat, but I don't really know anyone east of the ocean. I am an orphan and unlike the sojourners, I don't even have an extended family to return to.

These dreadful thoughts of loneliness filled my mind amidst Susan's cheerful voice proselytizing to me. I should mention that by this time, I've convinced Susan that I needed daily encouragement in 'The Word' or my ancestors would compel me to reject Jesus. After her work with The Navigators at handing out tracts near Chinatown, she would volunteer at the Women for Christ Centre. In the cool of the day, she would spend time in the Mission with me at the large table under the watchful eyes of the caretaker and other curious onlookers. We would read together. I would look up certain verses of the Bible the night before just so I could discuss with her. Sometimes the hateful Reverend Woods would join us.

Before sunset, she would leave for home in the Dolores suburbs, where she would also teach in the weekends. Those were days when I would miss her terribly.

One Friday afternoon was perhaps the coldest day in San Francisco. The overseas sojourners were celebrating the Winter Solstice Festival. I was depressed. Winter Solstice was a time of family gathering. When I was at the Lee Mansion, Old Ma would make glutinous rice for all the servants and father would be home the whole day and night. Not only that, I knew that Susan will be gone at least for a couple weeks with the coming Christmas season. I shivered my way to the Bible Mission not expecting her to be there. But seeing her lone figure lit a bonfire in my heart. The Mission was closed ahead of the holiday season. What shall we do?

I invited her into a Chinatown tea house. She readily accepted.

She was fascinated by everything, from the furniture to the tea itself. We decided that she wear a disguise. Her thrilled look was like a thousand sunbeams. She would wear a padded shirt over her blouse. I meekly suggested that she wore one of my black trousers and a fedora. She could only nod and grin excitedly. At the tea house, being I was worried as we were the one of two conspicuous customers that day. I started breathing only after the tea has arrived and the proprietor disappeared in the backroom to resume his Winter Solstice dinner with family.

Susan was puzzled.

"Well, where's the sugar?"

"Eh?"

"How can you not have sugar in your tea?"

"I will have absolutely no sugar in Chinese tea!" I declared indignantly.

She sipped her tea and put on an expression where her dimples depressed but not actually smiling- an inward smile.

"Well, I think this oo long tastes splendid; but would be better if there was some sugar in it."she added with finality. It was singular silly incident but it seemed uncover an irreparable rift between the two of us. It must be the Winter Solstice. I remember I was quite depressed for a while from that incident.

S's

It finally happened. Roger disappeared one day without a word. Her poor mother and that hateful Mary were frantic. I was surprised that I do not miss him at all. He was self-centered, arrogant, narrow minded man, and destined to fade from the life of Susan Milton. To my shock I have been writing more of Lee Seong more and more. Perhaps it was the amount of time we were spending together. Or the utterly fascinating things he tells me of Chinatown and China. Or perhaps it was the way he looks at me. I had discovered a side of Lee Seong I rather enjoy. He seems sincere, intense. When he speaks, it is with such deliberation and gentleness, if his back was to a vast universe of the unknown. Most importantly, I know that no matter what, he will stand by me.

I panicked the day Susan told me I was ready to 'graduate' from the new believers' class.

"We've covered the Believers' Prayer, the book of John, Paul's Letters. I think you are ready to discover the

Scriptures on your own, Seong." She was wearing a tulip colored skirt today with a tiny navy blue bow at her back. I gave her a brooch engraved with the Chinese character 'Snow' on her last birthday, which to my delight, she was wearing as well.

"So, no more classes?"

"No more classes."

"No more beginner's classes?" I corrected my self quickly

"No more beginner's classes."

"How about advanced classes?"

"Perhaps," she smiled mischievously. "But I think Reverend Woods would be more qualified to conduct that."

By now I caught on to the game.

"I guess I should write to Rev Woods immediately. God knows I'm excited to start advanced classes, with the Reverend."

"I think you should."

I put out my writing set and began to write; while stealing a glance up at her. She was neither smiling nor frowning. I had to give up.

"On second thought, I don't think the Reverend would be pleased with a Chinaman seeking guidance from him without any real grounding. Do you suppose you could afford more time from your busy schedule to guide through this intermediate period?" I looked at her with pleading eyes.

She looked as if she was about to burst out laughing.

"I think I can find it in my busy schedule; yes. Same time, same place?"

"So be it"

"I do still need to polish my Cantonese."

"That you do. Unfortunately, I am but a poor teacher"

"I think you're an inspirational one. Yesterday, I tried drinking tea without sugar. It was delicious."

She said the whole sentence in Cantonese.

1952

A customer came through the bookstore, interrupting my reverie.

"Excuse me sir, I am looking for thees book, called 'Mice and Men'…ah there it iz! Splendid. How much?"

No need for pidgin. Interesting.

As he proceeded to pay, I couldn't but notice the tattoo on his wrist. A man-made mark. His leathered skin and sallow expression confirmed it; signs of previous indescribable hardship.

"From Europe?" I asked.

"Yez, Germany,"

"You have one too" he smiled, looking at my right hand.

We did not exchange another word but had a wholesome conversation nonetheless. We shook hands.

I thought I would lose my right hand for good that day.

The famed Spanish Lane used to be a territory of Old Hwang that housed his busiest whorehouses and gambling dens. The lane behind it is where customers use to urinate in the middle of an exciting game. After collecting my days' wages, I chose to relieve myself along with other gentlemen that day. When I emerged, who should chose to appear but Syphilis Hung, flanked by two minions.

"The sins of the father, the son must pay," he grinned - a profound statement from one such as Syphilis Hung. I remember Susan mentioning something similar a few days ago although in a thoroughly different context.

I was terrified, and backed into the wall, stepping on my own urine pool.

"What you do to me, Brother Hung; Master Hwang will not approve," I pleaded.

"You are not a Lo Hup Tong member. I will beg forgiveness from Master Hwang after. He will not look beyond the principle of an eye for an eye." Syphilis Hung remarked with surprising clarity.

I have underestimated him. In spite of his animal-like behavior, it seemed Syphilis Hung had been planning revenge for a while. Just then out of the corner of my eye I spied one of his minions holding a red-hot branding iron.

Now I was completely fear stricken.

"Help! Help!"

"Hold him down."

His minions held my hands as he proceeded to apply an 'S' shaped brand onto my face.

"Better keep your mouth shut or it goes into your mouth"

In my struggle I managed to break free my right hand and instinctively covered my face. The iron landed on it. The pain was excruciating.

"Hold him tight you stupid son of a whore!" he yelled at his minion on my right.

My hand was forcibly retracted and I winced for the inevitable. My life flashed before my eyes but all I could think of at that time was Susan.

"Hey what are you doing!" someone from the main street shouted.

"Old Master! Someone is creating a scene in your territory!" followed by a commotion.

Old Master Hwang appeared.

"Ah Hung! Release him!"

That was the only authority that could command Syphilis Hung.

Old Master Hwang came over, inspected my injuries and declared,

"From today onwards, this vengeance is over. If anyone disagrees, it is a direct affront to me!" He walked away with Syphilis Hung meekly following, before throwing me a sneer.

I needed to get rid of this psychopath, and fast.

Susan fussed over my injury so much I was almost thankful to Syphilis Hung. I let her touch it and ran her finger all across the thick bandage that the herbalist applied on over a slab of pungent, brackish salve.

"A case of mistaken identity," I said. "Someone who looks like me apparently owed a lot of money to Old Master Hwang. And his henchmen took action."

"How could that even happen?" she asked incredulously.

"Well you know... all Chinamen look the same"

"That's not true."

"How many Chinamen do you know?"

"Well, only you....how many white girls do you know?

"Only you," I said quickly, with emphasis.

"How many Chinese girls do you know?"

Peach Blossoms flashed before my mind. No, she doesn't count.

"Not a single one."

"Is that right?"

"That's right, Susan Milton"

She smiled.

"Does it hurt still?"

"Very much so."

I think our relationship just reached another level that day.

When I took out my bandages three weeks later, a neat 'S' marked my palm.

"San Francisco Police Station"

"I need to speak with Chief Inspector Tucker please"

"Who're you?"

"Theodore Buzz from the Herald."

In the distance I heard "Hey Chief, it's that reporter again!"

Three minutes later, James Tucker's voice came on.

"Lee Seong. I hear you no longer work for Old Hwang. Congratulations. Stay clean and away from the old foxes. An educated man like you, what a waste. What do you have for me?"

"Old Hwang's men and Ip Chun from the Big Five are having a battle tonight at 11pm on the harbor front. The pretext is that it's over a girl. But the winner gets to control entire northeast side of Chinatown," I said, hurt by the insinuations.

"Why should we care?"

"Ip Chun hates you guys with a passion since one of you shot his son at point blank. If he controls the docks, there will be no more east-west cooperation that you enjoy with Old Hwang."

A pause, followed by a muttered curse.

"What do you want from this?"

"Old Hwang's right hand man, Scarface known to us as Fa Lau Hung, needs to be caught and deported."

"Yes we know Syphilis Hung. That's it?"

"It is but a humble request." I said, ready to disconnect.

"Hey Lee, hold on."

"Yes Chief?"

"The Chinese have a saying "Do not buy a hat that doesn't fit your head?"

"Something like that," I said simply.

"You may or may not have anything to do with O'Hara's death. I don't miss him but he's still one of us. I would advise Mr. Buzz that there will be hell to pay if he fails to differentiate friends and enemies," he said gently.

"Yes sair, I let the Mr Buss know this quick-quick sair."

None of my mails to Ah Yee have been replied. When I tried to solicit news from the backyard of the Lee Residence I found out that Old Ma has passed away. Ah Yat has married Peach Blossoms off to a rival family. No news of Ah Yee and his mother. Brother Robinson managed to meet up with him once in Guangzhou but after that there was nothing.

I was worried sick. As well, I mourned for Old Ma, my nursemaid. It was said that she only weighed four sacks of gunny rice her death. The gardener whispered to me Old Ma lingered for so long to wait for the arrival of her nephew from China. He was held up at Angel Island and was eventually deported back to China. That was the day Old Ma passed away. The Old Ma in my memory was a slightly overweight woman with rosy cheeks and strong fingers.

I was filled with gloom and despondence that morning as I walked into church for some spiritual solace. I caught Susan's eye and I winked and sat in the pew far back. She smiled back. I also caught the Reverend Woods eye as he climbed onto the pulpit. Not glancing at his notes, he began, after clearing his throat.

"The sixth chapter of Apostle's Paul's Second Epistle to the Corinthians thus read:

The Lord commanded us to not be yoked together with unbelievers. Or what fellowship can light have with darkness? Therefore come out from them and be separate, says the Lord. Touch no unclean thing, and I will receive you. I will be a Father to you, and you will be my sons and daughters, says the Lord Almighty. If there are amongst you who are being tempted to live in sin with a heathen…" he paused, his blue eyes bored straight at me. "Be on your knees and repent of your sins. The Lord God must be obeyed!" he thundered.

I was boiling with rage and walked out.

My anger simmered further when Susan appeared nonchalant the next day, as if she did not hear it, or that it did not apply to her.

"This Christian God…he is like a dragonhead of sorts, isn't he?"

"Lee Seong,! Of course not! God is all-loving, all-caring. How can you compare him to a dreadful underworld leader?"

"The dragonhead bestows kindness on whoever he wants and punishes whoever according to his justice system. His own people he treats like family. Those not in his tong, he smites. Isn't it the same? Tell me what's different."

Susan was silent for a while.

"God is the creator of all things; including all your dragonheads..."

"I bet he didn't create the Chinese or China...."

"No, all creation comes from God"

"But—

"Rev Woods--

"Ah, but you draw your knowledge from Rev Woods. What's so divine about that?"

Her eyes flashed with anger.

"I'm not sure why you are behaving like this to me..." she began in measured tones.

"Why does your precious Reverend Woods think the Chinese needs to be saved?"

At this point, I couldn't control myself.

"I think you're just being unreasonable," Susan said, closing her book.

"And if we're not saved like the white man, we deserve eternal fires of hell?"

"Are you saying my father and mother are roasting in the fires of hell?" I was getting louder.

"Well....the Bible says..."

"I know what the Bible says about that. The Dao De Ching also dictated that all souls will be judged by the God of the Netherworld. And the Dao De Ching was written way before the Bible."

Susan kept quiet, looking straight at me.

"Why? does my Confucianism offend you?"

"Stop it."

"Or my heathen way of speakee?"

"I said, stop it!" With tears in her eyes, she stormed out of the room; onlookers staring at me.

I closed my Bible, inwardly cursing myself.

I could not sleep that night; overcame with regret and fear that I could never see her again.

"Women trouble?" the ever perspicacious Masturbator Wang asked. He always asked that of everyone of everything they do.

To his surprise I said yes.

"Women are like that. Ignore them for a few days and they will come groveling at your feet"

Masturbator Wang's advice solidified my resolve. The next day, before the crack of dawn, I stole into Old Hwang's garden and pilfered some of his prized orchids and roses.

Then I waited in front of the Mission, not even sure if she would turn up today. It was chilly morning, a gentle breeze from the coast with an occasional gust.

To my surprise, there she was, earlier than usual.

"Hi," I walked up.

"Hello," she said. I could not interpret if the tone was seething or polite; or both.

" I"- we both began together.

"I"- we did it again. It made her giggle; and me, relieved. I gestured for her to go first.

She handed me the rectangular parcel she was holding. I eyed her questioningly.

"Open it"

"Here?" She nodded excitedly.

I gingerly opened the neatly packaged parcel by peeling along the folded lines, removed the packaging paper, and painstakingly folded it and returned it to her. Then I opened the box. It was a shiny black sombrero.

"Happy birthday, Lee"

I was suddenly ashamed of the flowers I stole for her. They seemed cheap, dirty and worthless in comparison.

"Are those for me?" she asked.

"Just my token of apology. I was extremely uncouth yesterday,"

"I'm sorry too."

We walked around the Mission along Stockton Street towards the town park, purposefully avoiding Chinatown. As we walked I poured out my life history to her, from the death of my father to the work I'm doing for Old Master Hwang. After that, we just walked silently.

It was only when we sat down on a bench that I finally and reluctantly released her hand. My hands were cold but hers were warm. We were both staring straight ahead. I stole a glance at her. Her cheeks were flushed pink from the chilly wind.

"By the way," she began.

"Yes?" I replied eagerly.

"Dao De Ching was written by Lao Tze. Not Confucius,"

"I know."

"Lee Seong. You are impossible."

"I know."

She laughed.

I smiled.

The Year of the Dog began in a somber mood. The festivities were toned down. The triad leaders kept to their own clans instead of hosting the annual festivities. The white constables who came for bribes were quickly paid, in auspicious red packets.

Two months prior, a group of tired-looking sojourners arrived in town; not from the port but from out west. They came without any possessions, some on horse carts, most by foot and claimed to have travelled more than a thousand miles. Old Hwang put on his best and assumed his de facto role as benevolent mayor. He invited all twenty eight of them to his Hall of Tranquility. It was a ghastly sight. The men were in all manner of decay. They had festering body sores, from unwashed wounds. They had the wide eyed stare of coal miners, unwashed and looked like walking corpses. In fact, the only way we recognized that they were Chinese were the queues that some of them managed to keep. Most of them seemed mentally deranged; repeating the same unintelligible words over and over.

When we finally managed to extract information from them, they were from different villages in Canton. They arrived at Golden Mountain more than seven years ago and were contracted to work in coal mines in a town that freezes in the winter and scorches in the summer about four days journey by train towards the west. The pay was good and there were plenty of work. Not all of them were miners. Some were shopkeepers, cooks, laundrymen, and barbers. One day almost without warning, a lynch mob descended upon them like 'enraged barbarians.' They were forced at gunpoint to leave. They did not know the fate of those who stayed but as they were fleeing, they were ambushed at every point to the railway station and were robbed of every trinket down to the shirts on their backs. All lost friends and families, to the back or front ends of rifles. They hid in the woods for a few days. Faced with starvation and sick with worry of those they left behind, they returned to their homes to find that the whole community was decimated, burnt to the ground. But before they could identify the charred remains of their loved ones, the mob descended on them once more. Out of a community of about two hundred Chinese souls, no one was sure how many survived.

"They did not just want to rob, they clearly wanted to kill, and torture!" one wailed.

Old Hwang closed his hands together and ordered that the men be fed and clothed and provided for. But I noticed his hands were trembling. So were mine. The men (the sane ones) got on their knees and kowtowed to him like son to father.

I scoured the English language press for news about the horrible massacre. There was only a short mention about a 'Chinamen disturbance' over in Wyoming. In Old Hwang's name, I wrote a long account of the massacre and sent it the Chinese Consuls in New York, London for what its worth, the Prefecture Government of Guangdong. Surely China cannot be that uninhabitable that they would prefer to be massacred here. Old Hwang, to his credit, approved of the letter in spite of the negative impact it might have on his business.

"Little brother, finally the white barbarians have revealed their bloodlust nature and unleashed their hatred on us Chinese," he said with a sigh. I remember feeling most alienated and desired to 'return' to China at that point; even Susan did not alleviate the unease. Indeed, the general air of urgency to leave the Golden Mountain was so palpable in

Chinatown; even the gambling tables and whorehouses were more quiet than usual. The only stall doing brisk business was Blind Man Kung, the fortune teller; who foretold a thin Wooden Rooster last year; many of whom attributed to the tragedy out west. Blind Man Kung was rarely wrong. Using the ancient art of divination, he could predict almost anything with startling accuracy.

The one time he was wrong, however almost cost him his life.

Blind Man Kung, of course; wasn't always blind. The older sojourners still referred him to his first nickname, Sprightly Kung. In his youth, like countless other impoverished youths he came to Chinatown to try his luck. Unfortunately, he had a deformed leg which was smaller and shorter than the other; necessitating him to use a pair of crutches to get around. He was in no shape to be a miner as his fellow countrymen rushed for the gold. But Sprightly Kung never let a mild inconvenience like that impede success. What he lacked in mobility he made up in showmanship and wit. Always dressed in simple ancient Taoist garb and cultivated a long flowing beard, he struck the figure of an ancient Immortal. The sight of him hobbling with his wooden crutch with an unearthly looking limb instilled a sense of awe and fear to the uninitiated. In time, he managed to secure a comfortable living as spiritual adviser for the rich barons, tong leaders and charged a dear price for his hidden wisdom and art of stealing a peek in the realms of the gods. One day an Old Master asked Master Kung to divine if he should prospect gold out west. Master Kung took account of the calendar, consulted the pagua, tong sing and divined that gold prospecting would indeed be a wise venture and the Old Master should make haste.

The expedition turned out to be a horrible disaster. The Old Master's only son was killed by white prospectors and all their equipment were robbed. So furious was the Old Master that Sprightly Kung became Blind Man Kung. Yet the families of Chinatown has a fairly high turnover rate, and the reputation of Blind Man Kung as a fortune teller soon recovered and this story was relegated to the stuff of legend or evil rumors. With the massacre at Wyoming, worried businessmen and housewives want some security against an uncertain future. What better security than a man who could peek into the future?

The Chinese sojourners have always treated their excursion here and tolerated hardship like they would back from their imperial lords. Throughout their lives, they've been told Chung Kuo, the Middle Kingdom is the center of civilization. From coolie to mandarin, there's a feeling of self-sufficiency. We have an ancient language, culture. All we need is gold. And after we have that, we are complete. There is no need to assimilate with barbarians. We just need to clench out teeth and work. Then we shall return home.

The Wyoming massacre made this return seemed all the more imminent. I imagined Chinatown devoid of anyone, a ghost town with empty shops and stray dogs gnawing at the charred human remains. I shivered at the thought.

Early one morning as I walked out of the Young Chinese Men Association, yawning as I went, my worst nightmare appeared before me. The whole of Chinatown Street was empty! A heavy anchor dropped in my heart as I ran to

Montgomery Street. Empty!

Grant Street. Empty!

It was as though everyone packed up and left for China.

I heard a commotion coming from Golden Mountain Alley. To my relief, I saw a crowd gathered there. I instantly guessed what happened. Sure enough, as I got nearer, there is was; a body hung from a telephone pole in front of Old Hwang's house. It was a Chinaman with a queue; and naked from waist down. As I got closer, I recognized the face. It was Ah Yat; dragon head of the Sam Hap Tong.

It was a war no one could afford to fight. No one could also afford not to fight.

The showdown between the Lo Hup and Sam Hup was much feared and anticipated. Businesses closed days ahead. Children were not allowed to as much put their heads out of the window.

Bookies were laying bets on who would be the winner.

The whole of Chinatown was sold out on hatchets and knives.

"Chief Inspector you have to stop this!" I was in front of James Tucker's desk.

"No I don't. Chinks' war has nothing to do with us."

"But Hwang's men didn't murder Ah Yat. Everyone in Chinatown knows it was his right hand, Fat Chen."

"We know but I don't care. When tongs go to war, it's you guys cleaning your own houses."

"There will be a massacre! Innocents might die," I pleaded.

"No can do Lee. The police force is paid for by the good tax payers of California. And you chinks don't pay a dime in taxes."

"What with you white men imposing the Exclusion Act on us? And killing us in Wyoming?"

"Get out of my office now."

I reported to Old Master Hwang what the cops thought.

He let out a long sigh.

"Then so be it. We go to war."

The battle began that afternoon on a dusty street. All businesses were closed, children huddled indoors and every window was clamped shut. Years later, there would be lores of extraordinary valor or an exceptionally good fighter who downed thirty or so enemies in seconds. The truth was that no one who witnessed the fight was alive after. I was at Old Hwang's side in his Bamboo Cane Restaurant which was triply bolted. We were surrounded by about twenty bodyguards with hatchets drawn, in case a legendary assassin from the enemy managed to barge in. Old Hwang tried his best to remain confident and nonchalant, going as far as making pretense of playing chess with the restaurant's proprietor. His fear was betrayed by the frequent spills when sipping his tea. At least thirty bodies and at least as many blood-stained hatchets laid strewn across the streets of Chinatown. Seeing that ghastly scene somehow brought about pangs of guilt in me. The sheer loss of life, the wanton brutality cried out for attention at my spirit which responded in an incredible burden of self-loathing. I recognized some as Old Hwang's henchmen who have been friendly to me. Instinctively I thought of Syphilis Hung; arrested by Tucker's men and deported to China; whom I have unwittingly spared from this gruesome fate.

Just two days ago, I was an impassioned negotiator with the white man' a mercenary doing Old Master Hwang's bidding. The passionate arguments I so deliberately crafted were meant to touch a man's heart, to induce guilt, regret, excitement or sadness so that he might do my bidding. Now the smell of death erased all my hubris. Any one of the dead bodies could be a Lee Kau with a newly orphaned Lee Seong. The dead faces, their unwilling ghosts, brought about memories of the starry-eyed sojourners in the boats; destined to work in a camp with conditions meant for animals; sojourners whose fate I helped facilitate. My ancestors looked upon me with sad disapproval. Jesus saw me clothed in sin; and I was ashamed.

The peace accord was hashed out quickly by Old Hwang and Fat Chen in the Bamboo Leaf teahouse. The sky was gloomy over the bloodshed the day before.

The two tong leaders were seated across each other in the teahouse; with their henchmen standing behind them, ready to spring into action if either party decided to initiate a surprise. Both sides have lost heavily. The compensation to the families of lives lost, the businesses that had to close and the risk of other tongs taking advantage of their vulnerability was felt more by Old Hwang, because the Lo Hup Tong was a bigger consortium; not to mention the loss of face. The peace agreement was a tacit admission that the Lo Hup Tong was responsible for Ah Yat's death, while the Sam Hap Tong had heroically avenged their dragonhead. But a prolonged war would literally destroy Chinatown; especially since the white cops refused to intervene.

As I was not a member of either Tong, I was 'invited' by Old Master Hwang to be a witness.

Hot tea was poured. My childhood nemesis Ah Chen has grown to be an adult version of the menacing kid bully that he was. Bearing tattoos of magnificent animals and scars of hatchet battles, he cut an intimidating figure in the underworld.

"Master Chen," Old Hwang saluted with his cup, making the first concession.

Fat Chen sneered. His plan has worked perfectly. The well-oiled business machinery of Old Hwang was not prepared for the classic Sun Tzu tactic of 'killing the goat to trap the tiger'.

Nonetheless, with the sole of his naked right foot resting on his seat, he picked his cup up carelessly,

"Master Hwang," he saluted.

They both drank.

Ah Chen was now the dragonhead of the Sam Hup Tong, with its territory expanded by concessions of the Lo Hup Tong. With it, Old Hwang lost monopoly of the human smuggling trade.

A written agreement of sorts was drawn up; insisted upon by the wily Master Hwang. He signed it in his neat, careful calligraphy. Fat Chen, who was illiterate, put on a show of reading it to save face. When given a brush, he went red with anger. He took a small knife, leading to bristling from Old Hwang's guards; cut his small finger and imprinted his blood onto the document.

Old Hwang smiled in satisfaction.

Pundits would later accord the final victory to Old Hwang. He had humiliated Fat Chen at that last moment. As well, the fine print within the agreement can be brought out at a later time to hamstring the Sam Hap Tong. That's why, they'll tell their children, even if you join the Triads, you must study hard to earn an education. After that I ran to the pier and vomited my guts out. I remember I trembled visibly for two whole days after; until I met Susan and told her everything.

S's

Roger is by now a bad memory. How I wish there are more boys as interesting as Seong. Shadowy intrigues, danger lurking in every corner, evil plots and ferocious Chinamen! Though we live not more than five blocks away, we live such different lives. Sometimes I feel sad for him. He looks so porcelain and delicate for such a life. Yet, admirably, he survives and thrives. It makes me conceited to think I am a source of comfort to him. I am quite certain by now he is in love with me. Love with a heathen Chinaman? Unthinkable!

With saved up money from my service with Old Hwang, I could now live in relative comfort, while writing occasional letters from concerned citizens to the real 'San Francisco Herald' as Theodore Buzz. I moved out of the Young Chinese Men Association and into single room hostel under the protection of Hung Hin Tong on the west side of Chinatown. The hostel catered for the passing-by Chinatown traveler, from merchants from China to low level dignitaries. Thus, there was a certain level of decorum. No opium smoking or prostitution was permitted for example. And the rooms have doors with locks. There was also centralized sanitary system instead of individual spittoon. The lobby occupies the whole ground level and all rooms were on the first floor. After setting up my late parents' altar, I furnished it with my books and bought a table to practice my calligraphy and writing. Since the massacre, amongst other things, I resolved to start journal, for whatever its worth.

Chinese couples never talk about love. Kung Fu Tze never expounded much on the love aspect between a man and a woman. The only women in Chinatown in those days were whores or middle-aged women. Though there were marriages and weddings, the match was set by their respective parents. Notions of love and romance I most gathered from my reading of western writings, and most from 'decadent' novels at that. The comfort I feel, the familiarity, the way she responded to me and I to her, is that love?

One day, I invited Susan to my room. After a moment's thought, she agreed. She would like to see my book collection. I beamed. She always seemed absolutely thrilled at the thought of venturing into the heart of Chinatown. I was more worried than excited and was especially concerned for her safety and my inability to protect her in the event that was needed. Again, I insisted that she wore a shawl, baggy clothes and black cotton pants to avoid suspicion. I heaved a sigh of relief when she was finally in my room without raising any eyebrows along the way.

Ever since we first met that day at Old Hwang's, I had struck up a friendship with Sebastian Chow; the Hong Kong Chinese who was educated by missionaries in Hong Kong and lived in Europe for a while. Expert forger, pianist, he also spoke and read French, Russian and Japanese, he told me fascinating stories of his experience with the British India Company. He was the only other soul whom I told about Theodore Buzz. He loved it and promised to incorporate me into a book he's writing about himself. When we conversed, we spoke only in English to avoid ears in the wall. When he had completed the job for Old Master Hwang, we promised to keep in touch. In every country he landed, he would send me a book.

My collection had by now reached about fifty books, all signed and marked by the date which I obtained them. I showed Susan my 'Count of Monte Cristo' given to me by Brother Robinson those many years ago. I even obtained a monograph from the popular Baptist preacher, Charles Spurgeon.

"Oooh! Spurgeon!" She exclaimed when she saw it like a little girl who saw a puppy or a nice dress at a window.

"May I?" raising an eyebrow.

"Please."

She took it out gingerly, opened with the first page with the greatest care and plopped on the only chair in the room; immersed in the book. I felt abandoned.

"I'll lend it to you," I said generously.

"Will you really? I'll take good care of it I promise." For that smile I would have given her China.

"I know you would. It is my latest and most precious book," I reminded her, hoping she knows that this means.

"Oh thank you so much. I've been waiting them to import his works here for so long," she looked at me with such gratitude I felt guilty that I never even read that blasted thing.

Since then, her visits became more frequent, till we abandoned meeting at the Mission Center altogether.

RAIN AND CLOUDS

It was about the seventeenth month since I met Susan. We have evolved into a couple or sorts. We would hold hands in secret. One rainy day I took her to my room to have tea and go over my books. Of course, we held hands. The rain was falling heavily on the zinc awning forming an orchestra that prevented her from leaving my side. But today something else was in the air. As we stood there hand in hand silently, by some magnetic power we became drawn to each other closer until out lips almost touched. Wide-eyed with amazement, I noticed Susan had her eyes closed as she too succumbed to this gradual corporeal magnet. At that very moment, a commotion was heard outside the window. I glanced downward to see two figures, one male and one female, both Caucasians strutting up towards the building. It wasn't long before I recognized the deep baritone booming voice.

"We want to go up! Up you understand?"

I quickly hid Susan in the room next door. It was door-less with only a thin sheet as partition, as it belonged to the caretaker.

Then I went down and stopped at the landing.

Reverend Woods was practically shouting, gesticulating with his walking cane at Old Liu behind the counter, who was half-trying to prevent this important looking white man from invading his space.

"Look man, do you want me to call the police on you? POLICE?!"

The poor old codger was visibly flustered. I could see he was torn between acceding to the angry white man's demands and alerting the Hung Hin Tong, which might create an international incident in these times. Reverend Woods was accompanied by a frumpy woman I know as Mrs. Beatrice, a deaconess; whom I only know by name because Susan mentioned she and her mother Rose did not see eye to eye on certain issues.

"Reverend Woods, what can I do for you?" I asked amicably from the staircase landing.

"You there! I know what you've up to, you monkey! Mrs. Beatrice saw you abducting Susan Milton to this building.

"Yes, Susan came here for shelter from the rain a while ago. But she soon left with an umbrella I loaned her. Did you not see her on your way going to alert Reverend Woods, Mrs. Beatrice?"

I delighted in seeing the sour scowl on the woman's face turned to self-doubt.

"I demand to see your room. If not, we will call the police," Woods wheezed.

I considered if I should flatly deny him and watch him weigh his limited options, especially since this is Chinatown. But then it would be Susan's reputation at stake. I nodded to Old Huang. With a huff, they both brushed pass me into my room. Once they went into my room, they tore open my cupboard, overturned my mattress and threw all my books onto the floor like maniacs, as if Susan could hide herself on a bookshelf.

The Reverend Woods pointed his cane at my nose.

"You stay away from our women, you hear that?" With that, the good Reverend and his scowling companion, left in a huff.

I quickly ran to the room next door to retrieve Susan, seemed composed and stoic but minutes later collapsed into a tearful outpouring.

"Oh, I'm so sorry Seong, I didn't know!" she sobbed. I've never seen my calm and collected Susan so emotional before. Nor I did mind in the least. In my world, every white man is a racist bigot until proven otherwise. In Susan's viewpoint, this truism is reversed. She seemed to be consumed by guilt at this presumed betrayal. I was secretly joyous but despondent at the same time. She fell into my arms and I instinctively wrapped my arms and patted her back as she sobbed. When the sobbing sobbed, we were like actors in a Beijing opera who found ourselves unwilling to leave the stage even though the ovation has died down. My arms remained around her. She did not seem to mind. Not knowing what else to do except that I should do something bold, I began to kiss her lips. Soon, her mouth parted and Susan kissed back.

PEACH BLOSSOMS BECOMES PURE JADE

When Ah Yat took over as dragonhead, Peach Blossoms was married to the Fourth Master of the Zheng Family, whose ancestor struck literal gold in Oregon decades ago and wisely invested the fortune into a diverse portfolio of sustainable income; their flagship business being teahouses. Indeed, the Bamboo Leaf; the rendezvous for Chinatown's upper crust was wholly owned by Old Master Zheng; who was also dragonhead for the San Luen Pong, a medium sized respectable tong that controlled a sizable territory.

Fourth Master was at the ripe old age of twenty by the time he was matched to Peach Blossom who was sixteen of age, a coup for both powerful Chinatown families.

The matchmaker heaved a sigh of relief when both families agreed to the union. It had taken her 10 long years to find a willing family for the Zheng Fourth Master; who although was from a wealthy, prominent merchant family; bore with him a generational curse.

Every single son of Old Master Zheng died in their sleep before their 23rd birthday. Master Zheng himself survived seven brothers; all of whom died at an unusually young age of unclear circumstances. Blind Man Kung told Master Zheng that the only thing he could do to ensure his progeny continues to survive is by accumulating karma by doing charitable works; in the hope that the gods might be touched and prevent the demoness from stealing his sons' souls. In any case if the gods chose to remain aloof, (as they often do) the demoness ought to be fooled by substituting his son's bed with a servant by the time they reached adulthood.

The Fourth Master was a man given easily to pleasures of the flesh. His parents could not bear to lose another heir and thus; if he had wanted the moon, by the gods he would have it. That said, he was a handsome lad; well-nourished with strong features. Thus, when the Fourth Master opened the veiled separated him and his wife, Peach Blossoms was pleased with what she saw.

Life at the Zheng Residence was not too different from the Lee's. There were servants for everything; the crème de la crème of Chinatown elite, if there was indeed such a thing. She was just expected to accompany her mother in-law at fan tan games occasionally and to show up at the family dinner table every evening. Two things were troubling to her at first. The first was that they had to sleep in a servant's bedroom. Even adorned with her own vanity set, it was still small and located next to the latrine. The second was the Fourth Master always slept in female clothes; to add another layer of deception to the demoness. She also hated it when the Fourth Master came home drunk and plunked his unwashed body beside her. At first, he was a loving husband and they spent many blissful nights together but as time and familiarity set in, he was back to his old haunts. Peach Blossoms was at first hurt by his whoring. But soon, she grew to accept it. These were some concessions that her mother in-law warned her about; and she agreed to it, after being offered a treasure box of jewelry imported from China. She didn't care that he didn't touch her much. Anyhow, if she was unhappy, there was always a nearby servant girl to pinch.

Peach Blossoms was convinced her life could only get better when the physician diagnosed her with pregnancy after feeling her erratic pulse. Many a precious gifts, ornaments and jade was showered upon her. Indeed, she was the most beloved sojourner mistress in the whole of Chinatown. When the baby was born, servants were sent to drag the Fourth Master from his cricket fight to see his son. Old Master Zheng threw a huge banquet, to celebrate his male grandson's 30th day of life, an affair comparable to the wedding not too long ago.

Old Master Hwang was invited, and it was then that I met Peach Blossoms after a long while. She was more beautiful than I remembered her. Her face glowed with contentment as she showed her infant son to relatives and well-wishers, her girly figure moved gracefully like a bamboo shoot in the wind. She pretended not to recognize me. The gifts from the well-wishers stacked up to the ceiling. There were jade and golden amulets, wild mountain honey from Taishan, birds' nest from Huangchou and wild ginseng from New York.

Two weeks after the happy event, Little Master Hwang was found by his nursemaid to be less active than usual. He would cry immediately after feeds and not before. In the next few days, he failed to respond to any stimuli and not moving his arms and legs. Every herbalist and physician in Chinatown were summoned. Even Blind Man Kung, who diagnosed an evil child spirit lurking about. For a handsome sum, he offered to perform an elaborate ceremony to evict the spirit. The whole Zheng household was in upheaval. Round the clock vigils were taken by relatives and servants voluntarily to look after the frail Young Master, who has since vomited everything he ate. Meanwhile, the servants whispered that the Fourth Master continued his cajoling and whoring.

On the 10th day after the symptoms began, the mischievous child spirit left and took the infant's life with him. Old Master Zheng was devastated. The Fourth Master was severely reprimanded and ordered to stay home to spend more time with his wife. Somewhat stunned by the death of his infant son, the Fourth Master turned over a new leaf and there was bliss in the Zheng household.

Unfortunately, all of Master Zheng's philanthropy, the room switching, the female clothing and the Fourth Master's rehabilitation failed to fool the demoness who had haunted the Zheng family for generations for on Mid Autumn's night; she claimed the life of the 4th Master shortly after the grand celebration of his 24th birthday. Peach Blossoms woke up that morning, greeted her in-laws and reported that her husband was still resting from last night's exhaustion. She returned to the bedroom in the evening to find that she had spent the night with a corpse.

The grief-stricken Zhengs; ashamed to admit at last to a generational curse, turned their confusion to anger towards their young daughter in-law. Peach Blossoms was demoted to a servant girl. Her kindly mother in-law dropped her kindly façade and started to abuse her. One night, while she was washing her mother in-law's bound feet, she forgot to mix cold water into the basin with the scalding water. Old Mistress Zheng yelped in pain. Peach Blossoms was given twelve lashes of the bamboo in the family hall as she knelt before her late husband's altar. Her tearful messages for help to the Lee residence were not answered. One night, Peach Blossoms, filled with hatred and sorrow, ran away from the Zheng residence with the help of her former sympathetic servant-girl.

Knowing she would need to escape the length and breadth of Master Zheng's reach, Peach Blossoms ended up on the edge of Chinatown, a shanty street whorehouse named Sally's, shared by both Orientals and whites alike from the nearby work camps. Sally-Mae, the keeper of Sally's saw marketed her enterprise as a 'respectable saloon', with 'spirits and gentlemen's liquor' for the working man to enjoy and unwind'. Her girls are usually live-in though some travel with the weekend piano-and-guitar band from Los Angeles. Though business was brisk, she suffered endured heavy competition from other saloons, dance halls, music houses, bars of other variety and exotic attractions for the working man. Her shrewd eye immediately saw the potential in the allure of an Oriental girl to beat the competition. As well, chinks work for half wages. That's the rule.

Hungrily chomping on the hard bread; the first she's ever tasted, Peach Blossom knew it would an expensive meal as she looked at the greedy eyes of the fat woman with blotchy skin, huge breasts and greasy yellow hair before her.

It was said that Little Peach Blossoms did not utter a single word in the two years she slaved at Sally's. No complaints, no protests. White, Mexican, Chinese, she served them all.

One perspicacious Chinese customer recognized the pale skin without blemish indicative of a life spent indoors, the smooth hands foreign to manual labor, and the hollow eyes of indescribable trauma and surmised her background. But as much as he tried, he could not induce Peach Blossoms to say a single word. He tried coaxing her, paying her money, slapping her but she was like a rag doll, a soulless body. Giving up, he lit up his pipe. That seemed to elicit a glint in Peach Blossoms' eyes, and he offered it to her, a mixture of opium and tobacco.

Before he left, she tugged at his sleeve and said 'more'.

It was the day deep in winter when the whites celebrate their religious festival of a god who was born this day thousands of years ago. The whorehouses were usually empty. Yet Sally's was always open. The heathen had the right to entertainment, even if it was Christmas. The whites who were at a whorehouse at this time are those with no families, hard men who had forgotten all about fear and decency. One such man was nursing his whisky at Sally's when he noticed Peach Blossoms drowsily emerged from the toilet. His lust aroused, he paid Sally and stumbled his way to her room. Sally was about to protest but laid her eyes on the gleaming gold and shrugged.

Peach Blossoms hands were shaking. She wished the Chinese customer would come back soon with her opium. It has been thirty-six hours since her last dose. When the large white man barged in, she rolled her eyes and just gestured towards the bed. In his drunken state, he ejaculated after not more than three thrusts and became limp. Unsatisfied, he kicked her onto the floor, pulled her hair violently and turned her around and tried to enter her unnaturally. But tried as he might, he could not achieve an erection. He decided to substitute his penis with an empty whisky bottle. Peach Blossoms yelped in pain. All of a sudden, that seemed to unleash all her pent-up hatred, the injustice she has suffered. The Peach Blossoms, Princess of Old Master Lee, the Thief of my heart in my childhood screamed from within the hollow husk that was her body. In addition, her opium longing infused this rage with supernatural strength. With all her might she pushed the man away and grabbed the nearest object, a mirror with a metal frame and brought it down on the man's head. The metal stayed lodged in his skull so deep, Peach Blossom was not able to attempt a second blow.

When her mind cleared, she realized enough what she had done to leave the scene immediately. And ran she did. Little Peach Blossoms climbed through the window and ran with all her in her nightclothes without shoes along the main road towards the bright horizon, hoping she would find her papa at the end. The light at the end never did seem to get any nearer, and she collapsed. When Peach Blossoms came to, she thought she had died. Her surroundings were all white. There were other people moving about silently, all dressed in white as well. Her clothes were also as snow. She was jubilant and immediately got up to look for papa. As soon as she climbed out of bed she fainted again, much to the horror of the nurses.

Peach Blossoms had collapsed on Brennan Road, deep in white territory. She was found by a late-night coachman and sent to the nearby hospital for unwed mothers, run by the Sisters of Immaculate Conception.

When she was more alert, Peach Blossoms seemed to be in another world. This was not Chinatown. Surely, she didn't run that far. Did anybody know what she did at the whorehouse? Did anybody even know who she was? Nobody spoke Chinese here. She started to panic. But she kept it to herself. And when anyone asked her a question, she remained mute.

The Mother Superior was a good friend of Rose Milton; whose intrepid daughter was known to speak the Chinese tongue. Susan promptly arrived to a Peach Blossoms who was sitting on her bed hugging her knees, staring at the blank wall. Her breakfast laid untouched on the table.

"She kept trying to kill herself. First, she tried to jump out the window, then she tried to cut her wrist with the utensils." the nurse told Susan who noticed the scars on both wrists. "We wanted to put her in a straitjacket but the matron said to try you first." Susan thanked the nurse.

"Lei ho ma?" she asked. how are you

Peach Blossoms turned to the familiar tongue and the strange face that spoke it. After Susan introduced herself with her then flawless Cantonese (if I may say so myself), Peach Blossoms burst into torrential tears.

Susan only achieved in that and getting her to start eating on the first day.

It would be many days later before Peach Blossoms finally could find her words to piece the tragic story of her life. For the next few weeks, Susan visited Peach Blossoms every day. Two long months passed before she could smile.

When Susan told me the story, I scoured the newspapers and couldn't find any news of the murder.

"Detective Gould speaking," an impatient, scratchy voice came on.

"Hello, Theodore Buzz from The Herald." A sigh followed by a barely audible curse.

"I'm calling to follow on the murder of a man down on Sally's about a month ago."

"What about it?"

"Have you found the culprit? The good people of North End are concerned about a murder that happened in a place they visit so frequently."

Sarcasm was lost on Detective Gould.

"Killed by his whore but Sally Mae ain't ratting her out; except that from loud noises heard seemed he was abusing her. The dead body matched a description of a runaway miner we were looking for last month. Robbed a bank out in

Palo Alto and raped several women there too."

"Is there a manhunt going on for his killer?"

"You don't have ears? I said the investigation was closed. The police do not waste time solving deaths of fuckin' rapists."

"May I quote you sir?"

"Don't you dare, you son-of-a-bitch. What's your name again?"

I hung up and cursed myself for not stopping myself with that last comment. That agitated cop might get suspicious and remember the conversation.

When I relayed the news to Peach Blossoms via Susan, she was so relieved her whole body shook. It took weeks but eventually, she recovered from her shock somewhat, but Peach Blossoms remained mute and observed to stare at a blank wall for hours on end. The kindly Sisters fussed over her incessantly, like a little mute lost kitten. But Peach Blossoms would only light up when Susan visited her and spoke her tongue.

One day, Peach Blossoms tugged at Susan.

"Snow Mountain, I would like to know this Jesus God of yours"

"I didn't even ask her. I didn't give her any tracts. It was the work of the Holy Ghost." Susan would explain to me later in excitement, before I could tease her zealous proselytism.

Susan patiently explained to her the various tenets of faith, the story of the birth of Christ and men's salvation as she did with me before. And then she led her in the Sinners' Prayer.

"A new life? Is that really possible?" asked Peach Blossoms tearfully.

"Yes, the old is past now, Peach Blossoms," said Susan.

She became thoughtful. "No," she said. "Peach Blossoms was a nickname given to me by my mother. That was my old life. My real given name is Pure Jade. Peach Blossoms is dead now."

And so Pure Jade became somewhat of a member at the convent, participating in Mass and helped with housekeeping. Still, she kept to herself and refused English lessons that Susan offered. One cloudy night, a scream was heard emanating from the convent. A young nun found Pure Jade preparing to hang herself from a tree in the lawn. Susan Milton was immediately summoned.

"Will God forgive me? Even though I've killed someone?" Pure Jade asked tearfully, as my kindly Susan administered to her.

"Yes, God promises that in His Word"

"Even if that someone is innocent?" she asked.

"The blood of Christ washes away all sins. Besides, that man was doing unspeakable things to you"

"No, not that animal! Not that animal" Pure Jade continue to wail.

Pure Jade revealed that soon after she left the Zheng's, she found out that she was pregnant again. Her tiny frame allowed her to hide her pregnancy until term; when she delivered a baby boy in the latrine of Sally Mae, all by herself. As she gazed at the fragile infant, it seemed to morph into the mocking face of a sneering Fourth Master. Then to her horror, there was a tube leading from the infant's belly that was attached to a mesh of substance that seemed to resemble the form of a demoness. In a surge of fear and hatred, she wrapped the infant in bloody newspapers and left it in the sewage tank. After she told her story, she began sobbing uncontrollably.

Susan just hugged her.

And that is the story of Sister Pure Jade; the Angel of Chinatown who perished in the San Francisco Earthquake twelve years later while rescuing trapped children from an orphanage.

A CHINAMAN'S LOVE

Since Pure Jade's episode, Susan and I got a lot closer. Our kissing sessions became more frequent, passionate and spontaneous after that rainy day. I made doubly sure she didn't do it out of spite against Rev Wood that first time.

One day in our Bible study sessions, (Susan still insisted we do them) we reached 1 Corinthians 13

"Susan, what is love?" I blurted out.

She flushed.

"It says here Love is patient, love is kind.."

"No, I mean, what IS love?"

She stopped and stared straight at me.

"What do you mean, Lee Seong?"

"I think I love you," I said simply; not quite expecting what she would do or say. I felt like I just dived into the Pacific Ocean without knowing how to swim, waiting for a boat to rescue me or sink to the bottomless dark below.

She was quiet for a long while. I held my breath.

"I love you too," came the whisper.

So, that feeling of rising from dark waters and into the sky...that's love. And no, those kisses were not out of spite.

The following week we found ourselves next to each other in Susan's parlor. I was in a tweed suit several sizes too large. Susan was holding my hand. Her mother's eyes were piercing through as if to extract our hands from each other with her steely gaze.

"Well, I never," her lips moved ever so slightly, shaking her head.

"Well, ma'am, I would like to ask you for your daughter's hand in marriage." I said.

"Mr. Lee. I am going to be very frank with you," her diction was precise. "I know this day was coming. I just did not expect it so soon. Knowing my daughter, I know my opinions only play a nominal role and I shall keep them to myself. Your life together would be unbearably hard but I'm sure Mr. Lee; intelligent man that you are, you are most aware of that already."

"Yes, ma'am. I do indeed"

It didn't sound like a blessing to me. Neither was it a refusal. She finished her tea, signaling the end of the interview. It did not take long for the First Baptist congregation to hear of our union. I was exceedingly worried about the scandalous repercussions. Many unkind words drifted to my Chinese ears and western mind.

"Are you sure you want to marry me, Susan Milton?" I asked suddenly.

Tears brimmed in her eyes.

"What are you saying?"

"Your Mother is not very approving."

"It's not because you're Chinese" Susan said. "It's because she'd rather you have a family, some sort of...stable background."

"Like a white man?"

"Well, no, yes. Either way, it's not your race. Mother made it very clear to me. She was just unsure on how to communicate it with you"

"Saying that she 'has reservations' has conveyed it very clearly I think"

"She's not ecstatic but I'm the one getting married, not her."

I thought about my father.

"Perhaps you should listen to your mother," I don't know why I said that. Susan was wise to not respond to that.

"Chicken-fart egg of a whore!" she expelled in Cantonese; slamming her fist on the table, thinking she uttered the Chinese counterpart of 'fiddlesticks!'

I could not help but laugh.

"Lee Seong, do you want to marry me or not?"

I broke out of my spell and looked her. She looked cross with her hands on her hips.

"Yes!" I said without a moment's hesitation to the woman of my life.

Marriage!

"If you ask me, a man must have control over his woman at all times. If you are rich and powerful like an Old Master then it comes naturally. But if you're a poor egg like me, then marriage is suicidal," said Masturbator Wang sagely; sitting cross-legged smoking his cheap cigarettes. "Because while we men become dragons as we grow older, women are hens. And the worst think that can happen to a man is becoming a hen-pecked husband." I was back at the Young Chinese Men Association hostel to run an errand for Old Hwang and exchanged news with my old roommates. I let it out that I was getting married but no one suspected it was to a Caucasian woman.

"So, Masturbator Wang, your hen thinks you're a dragon? That's not what Big Breast Lin told me!" Someone from the far corner of the room shouted, to howls of laughter.

"That whore, I'll teach her!" More laughs and hoots. I don't even know why my mind somehow labeled

Masturbator Wang as an authority for marital issues.

Reverend Brown declined to conduct the wedding service for us. Rose had insisted that we asked him anyhow. In a telephone interview with Theodore Buzz about his evangelistic work in Chinatown, he disclosed that he could not condone a marital union between a white and an Oriental, especially if the Oriental is the man. "The chink culture is just too different. It will only serve to dilute our superiority". Theodore Buzz promised not to publish that last off the cuff comment.

I told Old Master Hwang I wished to venture out of Chinatown to try my luck. The old man took news of my leaving his service slowly.

"That is good. But I hear a rumor you are going around town with a white woman."

I stood, waiting for him to finish his tea.

"Though we are a thousand li from home, remember that dragons can only be matched with phoenixes. Your parents are no longer in this realm. I am perfectly willing to be in their stead and find you a good woman. The barbarians are good for a little release every now and then. But there's no need to be unfilial and offend your nine generations of ancestors by marrying a white bitch."

My father's words about Old Huang echoed in my mind. 'old sly fox' ' never trust him' 'don't turn your back to him'. This human smuggler's disapproval was the clearest sign that my father would bless my union with Susan.

I thanked Old Master Hwang, accepted his generous blessing of fifty dollars and used it to pay advance rent for our little apartment on Montgomery and Market St. on the outskirt of Chinatown. It was the perfect spot. To the right, is the financial world of the west, where suits and bowler hats bobbed on the streets on a busy day. To the left was Chinatown where queues, sharp Cantonese sounds, and aroma of roasted entrails emanate day and night.

To say I was nervous before the wedding would be an understatement although I am sure I would never admit to it then. Once the auspicious date was decided, I swore a mui po who doubled as a 'mistress of ceremony' to secrecy, I took her to see my 'unusual' bride. She stepped back in horror when she saw Susan and insisted that my parents be informed about this. She was only appeased when Susan spoke with her in Cantonese and her familiarity with the various customs that I've coached her. And also the double payment I promised her. We bowed before my parents' ancestral tablet and offered tea. I promised Susan one day we will have a western ceremony. Before she left, the mui po asked for our zodiacs. I was a Monkey and Susan, a Rat. The mui po gave me strange look and left without another word. Haunted, I secretly consulted the tung sing (almanac) I always kept within my bible. It said Rats and Monkeys were not ideal life partners. I threw it out.

On the night of our wedding, I presented a surprise gift to Susan. It was a red cheongsam. We shared a cup of wine and fed each other cold dishes on the table.

Then I led her to our marital bed.

I began to feel nervous. Aunt Feng came darting into my mind. I could not feel an erection! Susan kept her eyes on the floor.

'This is going to be a disaster,' I wailed privately. I unbuttoned the first few buttons of her cheongsam and stopped. Accusations narrated by the voice of Masturbator Chan darted in my mind like poisoned arrows.

'The husband who cannot satisfy his wife deserves to be cuckolded!'

I tried to bring up memories of how I've imagined Susan naked so many nights.

'A man's erection is the measure of worth in the eyes of a woman in heat!'

Damn you Masturbator Chan!

'A man can be a loser at work; but must be king in bed!'

Susan took my hand and led me away from her dress. I felt defeated. I climbed onto bed; my mind on my limp penis. Behind me, Susan blew out the candle and climbed in after me. I was lying on my back and dared not face her.

"What's the matter, Old Master?" she asked every so tender, in Cantonese. In the dark lying side by side, while holding hands, I told her about the incident with Aunt Feng. We laughed. Then she confided in me in tears that she thought I wasn't attracted to her; that her Caucasian features were ugly in my eyes when I hesitated. I assured her that was not the case and we kissed in the familiar way we knew so well. At that exact point in time, I felt incredibly aroused. From then on, we stopped talking and just move smoothly, anticipating each other's moves as though rehearsed; undressing each other and moving rhythmically like the tide of the sea and gathering of the clouds until we climaxed; when at last the rain poured.

That was the period in my life when I was completely at peace with the cosmos. The White-Chinese duality I carried was most insignificant. Life was full of hope; the future held nothing but a welcoming bright light. One of the changes I embraced with caution was fashion. Western dresses; in my mind were very uncomfortable consisting of multiple layers of impractical garments. Chen Ping oft-used advice "Just get used to it" echoed in my mind as I started wearing tailored khakis, shirts, coats, socks and substituted my airy canvass shoes for leather ones. All these were minor inconvenience when I woke up in the morning and the first person I saw was Susan. It was as though we've known each other all our lives.

I applied for the position of sub-editor for the San Francisco Star; which had an office just one block from where we live. Dressed most uncomfortably in a western suit and tie, which Susan assured me was most resplendent, I walked right into the Chief Editor's office and inquired about the opening.

"Where did you learn how to speak English?" he asked when we were seated, glancing up from my essays.

"From a white man when I was young, and later at the University of California."

"Doesn't say here you went to university," he said, gazing at my resume. "Did you write this too?"

I sighed inwardly.

"Yes sir, I did. I didn't finish sir, my sponsor withdrew."

He gave an inscrutable grunt.

"Are you married?"

"Yes sir; it's been six months now."

He raised an eyebrow.

"She was also born here; before the Act came into effect," I answered truthfully.

"Ah," mildly embarrassed that I answered the unasked question.

"This is really well-written," he was reading 'The Plight of Chinese Americans – by Lee Seong'

"Thank you," I muttered. A prolonged silence as he continued reading.

"Well Mr. Lee. Folks around here say a lot unkind things about your kind. But I know you Mongols are as intelligent as any other. Welcome to the San Francisco Star."

We shook hands.

S's

Marriage!

It seemed like such a big step from when Seong said 'I love you,' (the only man who've said that to me) yet everything happened so quickly. I love the way he fussed over things and took pains to ensure I was comfortable. What a remarkable Chinaman. My husband.

5 January 1874

I left Chinatown just in time it seemed. The tong wars erupted in full force, as resources become scarce and human smuggling became the prime source of income. Almost every week, there was a violent incident in Chinatown. The Young Chinese Men Association was burnt to a crisp in the middle of the day. Fortunately no one was in the upper storey at that time. There was one death. It was probably Old Lam. I made a conscious effort to not be aware of Chinatown goings-on. The San Francisco Star spanned three stories and occupied two whole lots. In the afternoon, I would indulge in a cup of tea on the rooftop; even when it drizzled. It overlooked both Chinatown and Union Square; and gave one an impression of standing an imaginary line dividing east and west.

"Lovely day,"

I turned around, surprised. It was a clean shaven young man in a brown cap whom I recognized as one of our cub reporters.

"I'm sorry to interrupt your thoughts. Think I'll be going," he said shyly.

"By no means. I'm sorry I am not able to offer any tea. Please, some company is always welcomed."

"Oh I am just up here to scout for the Fook Wah Funeral home. I need to do a cover story about the opium bust there this afternoon."

"I can show you," I pointed out the distinct building and wrote out the Chinese characters for him. He was grateful.

"So, when do you get to be full-fledged?" Cub reporters at The Star has an indeterminate period of internship.

"Well, I haven't really told anyone this; but I hope to be a writer one day."

"A wordsmith! A very good vocation. Words can tear a wound deeper than a bullet, lift a man's spirit better than whisky and be more destructive to a community than an earthquake." Tea always makes me wistful.

"I never really thought about words that way. To be honest, I just thought it would be grand that many people could read what I want them to"

"It is grand. A true privilege and a position of power."

"What should I write about?"

"When I was learning English, my first book was the Count of Monte Cristo, translated from French. I've read it at least twenty times and each time was like the first. It was a book of wealth, adventure, intrigue, romance...things that most if not all of its readers never could to experience in their lifetime. People love it for precisely that. They are elevated to a pristine plane of their sweetest dreams. The true challenge is to write a book of the downtrodden, the poor and the disenfranchised. And paint a picture of ennui that emanates a thousand colors. About people who are breathing and speaking but have no voice. To indict your reader of their misery and endear them to its; that's true genius," my voice trailed off as an afternoon cloud loomed over Chinatown.

"Like stabbing a man and he still respects you," the young man pondered.

"Exactly."

"Is that why you work for the newspaper?"

I laughed "No. Chinaman work only to survive. Just wan to makee the mar-nee!"

It was his turn to laugh.

It was the end of lunch.

As were parting way, he asked, "Sir, what's your name?"

"Lee"

"John." We shook hands.

"Have we met before?"

He laughed. "I wasn't sure before but now I am. Remember a certain donkey cart ride into San Francisco?"

It seemed that after dropping me off, Jarvis' family arrived in Salinas and after an arduous decade of harsh conditions and tribulations, made it as a dairy farmer. Emily died a year after we parted of a severe disease of the bone marrow. Gwyn recently got married to a cotton wealthy farmer in Salishaw.

We exchanged addresses and promised to keep in touch.

For two blissful years I only ventured into Chinatown during festivals or at Susan's behest. Thus I was shocked to bump into Old Master Hwang one day in the unlikeliest of places – the front door of the San Francisco Star office. He was wheeled-in in a wooden wheelchair by an aide. The toe on his right leg was wrapped in thick bandage with the familiar odor of Chinese herbs. The security guard was refusing him entry. The old fox was scowling contemptuously.

Years of fine living and heavy drinking had taken a toll on his body. His abdomen was bloated. His skin was pale with tortuous veins over his face. When he spoke, it was with such effort that every word seemed to be plucked from the top of a mountain. The old fox was no longer wry and formidable and seemed more like a sick bear. Most ostensible, he was miserable and lonely, manifested by new creases across his forehead. I secured entry for my former patron and helped him translate. He wanted to put an advertisement for his missing son. It was his third son; Name of Hwang Lu-Ping; 18 years old. Last seen 2 months ago on the outskirts of Chinatown with a dark-skinned woman and several white men. He insisted several times that his own name be inserted prominently so that the kidnappers would who they are dealing with and that if his son were to return safely, there would be no reprisals; only reward. I've never seen the old fox of Chinatown in such a state of anxiety. His face had a certain pallor that suggested his appointment with King Yama was imminent. What would Chinatown be without the likes of Old Master Hwang?

During these turbulent weeks, I received a surprise: a letter from Ah Yee; written with his familiar script.

Most dear brother Seong,

I must humbly beg your forgiveness for not writing earlier.

On board the ship, we were robbed. We arrived in China without money or possessions. When we arrived at my mother's family, her father was displeased at our disgraced state. My own grandfather turned us away. For the past four years I toiled as a manual laborer; carrying sacks of gunny I never thought I could muster.

One day the Old Master noticed that I could read, write and count and I became his foreman. How I appreciate the noble efforts for Master Liu! I am filled with shame to think we called him Four-Eyed Frog. (I hope he is well). To cut a long story short, I now own the Mei Tin Rice Factory.

I don't know why I did not write to you all these years. Perhaps I was really that busy. Or perhaps I was ashamed. The burden of Second Master was a poison.

I think about papa a lot and hope his health is good. Do tell me about him and Peach Blossoms in your next letter, won't you? Mother's health has deteriorated somewhat but this un-filial son can at least provide a comfortable life. She keeps asking about papa. But I don't think I will ever make that trip as long as Mother is alive.

Now that I've really arrived, so to speak, I am starting to miss you and our carefree childhood. I've gotten news about you from Brother Robinson. A foreign university! You have done our family proud.

I heard news from the Consulate that times are getting harder for Chinese in the Flower State. I expected to see only Chinese in China but there is a great expanse of land that is inhabited solely by yang ren in Guangzhou. Not unlike Chinatown; even the fact most of us are afraid of them here;

just like in Chinatown. But I think you would be able to navigate that you could speak that devilish tongue. If you are ever here, I implore you to write me.

By the way, I am now married with 3 children. My wife is a native of Fujian from a family of scholars. How are you doing in this regard? I hope to hear from you soon. Do not emulate this brother in writing so sparsely.

Yours brother

Ah Yee

I wrote back immediately.

I now come into contact with many non-Chinese in my work; white folks who resembled more the ones from the university; equipped with an education and a complex dilemma about the Chinaman. I remember thinking long and hard one day after reading The Workingmen Committee of California pamphlet sent to the bureau titled 'The Chinese Must Go!' which was also the platform for the leading mayoral candidate. I struggled internally to write a reply and rebuttal to the pamphlet but eventually decided against it. At that time, it felt like pushing against the waves. Chinatown seemed like a fungus growing conveniently on a grand oak tree which no longer welcomed it. I finally accepted that Chinatown one day will lie fallow. The sojourners will all return to China. And half-way Chinamen like me will be left to fend for ourselves. I also now have more access to information about the rest of America. It seemed there were many different voices far away from California advocating on behalf of the Chinese. The chaotic diversity of intellectual and political climate made me comfortable.

Marital life with Susan has proven everything I learned about sex before was baloney.

"Husband, what goes on in your mind after you climax with me?"

"What kind of question is that?

"Just answer it"

I thought a long while.

"Bliss...then poetry"

"Poetry? Lee Seong, you simply must tell me!"

Drawing a deep breath, I begun in English

On the bed we embrace through silk

And dance like Mandarin ducks with twined necks.

Like two kinds of jade, we go well together,

Through her dark eyebrows knit frequently in shyness.

We began to caress each other as I continued,

She feels strengthless, unable to move even a wrist, though she's so sensitive that her body tenses. The light of her sweat is like pearls. Her tangled hair is loose and hazel. Happiness like this comes once in a thousand years.

She seemed happy with my answer and showed me that she was. An ancient Chinese poem making a Caucasian woman of the 19th century aroused. It was a moment to remember.

I noticed that Susan has been praying more and more fervently. In the morning I would wake up seeing her on her knees. She would spend hours at night pouring over the Bible. When we go to Service on Sunday, I would wait for her hours after service whilst she counseled with the minister.

My irrational mind began its tortuous imagination. Is she thinking of becoming a nun?

I quickly chided myself for even thinking that. Susan has always been religious. It's that part of her that attracted me, I reminded myself.

Perhaps what she needs is to be a mother. It had been two years but Susan hasn't been pregnant. Is there a lower likelihood for a Chinaman to impregnate a white woman? The very notion seemed ridiculous but I could not be absolutely sure. Susan thought the question was ridiculous too. But her reasoning was based on some extrapolation from the Bible. She admitted she has never seen a mixed raced child before.

Theodore Buzz wrote in on a Sunday edition of The Star as a concerned citizen; highlighting the possibility of a mixed race generation; in view that America now has the most diverse population in the world. Scots-Irish, White-Indians, White-Black. etc The readers' replies were nothing short of ferocious. Many threatened to boycott the Star. Two letters threatened to burn us down.

The Chief told me that the loony Theodore Buzz's letters should never be published again.

Another change that overcame Susan was that she spoke almost no English with me. When I got home from work, I was greeted by a Chinese woman with blue eyes and brown hair. Dinner consisted of only Chinese dishes. Even the English ditties she used to sing while moving about the kitchen changed to Chinese rhymes.

"Susan, I feel like having rhubarb pie today,"

"No husband you don't. I still remember your expression when you first had rhubarb pie," she put on that hidden smile again. It was true; the intoxicating sweetness with a careless slab of sour was one of the most objectionable stimuli to my taste buds. I had tried quickly to mask my disgusted look to avoid embarrassing Susan but it only made things worse. Luckily for me, she just laughed.

"Well, we don't need to eat rice every day," getting to the point.

"What's wrong with it?"

"Because you never ate a single grain of rice before you married me. One day, you will get tired of being Chinese. Then you would not love me anymore." I don't know why I revert to this child-like behavior, but it seemed so natural at that time. It was as if Susan and I were trying to live our lives as adults but wanted catch up our lost childhood together.

"Well, if I ever do then we can have rhubarb pie," She replied primly, in the most delightful fashion.

1953

"The good old days" seemed to be common catch phrase these days; uttered by young runts barely qualified to use the phrase; yet given the choice, these folks would rather live in the present if not the glittering future; atomic bomb or not.

The truth is, the old days were hardly good; collectively for mankind and every person honest to himself. The first fifty years of a man's life is always a tale of struggle, tribulations and suffering. And it is with this sober reminder I search my mind for unpleasant memories about Susan and I during that time.

I could not find any.

S's

1875 December 10

He grabbed me from behind a tree. I gasped in horror, quickly turning around to see if anyone noticed. No, of course not. He'd planned this meticulously; every time, for the last three months. From the rude surprise to the dilapidated room in the abandoned building on Nob Hill, filthy save the bed, almost certainly prepared by him. He then put his hands so petulantly under my skirt. He was rude, invasive, ferocious, almost. I pushed him away, but he seemed possessed, and it was inviting. When he pulled me into his dilapidated room, I was in a daze, like lamb being led to a slaughterhouse; but inner part of me wanted to be slaughtered, and enjoyed being so.

He breathed heavily down my neck, reeking of tobacco. I had dreamed of this ever since I was a girl and saw him for the first time in church. In my prayers, I would be married to Roger and be his woman. In my dreams he would be doing exactly this to me every night. It felt so wrong now but who would want to stop one's wildest dream becoming true? I attempted to push him away to silence the nagging voice of guilt, but it was the loud and firm voice of desire that had the greater effect. His mouth devoured my breasts as if he would really. When he entered me, my body erupted like a geyser. It lasted no more than ten minutes and it was over. And then we laid intertwined in each other's arms, naked in shame for the world to see; another brazen audacity for with my husband, we always did it underneath the sheets. Suddenly I was awashed with guilt; as though struck by lightning and started weeping.

I wished I had to courage to kill myself.

"Get out! He left with a grin and without a word. I spent hours with my head buried in the sheets in that dilapidated room wishing the earth would open up and swallow me. I know that in time, this dastardly pattern would repeat itself. I would spend the next few days praying fervently for the Lord's forgiveness. Then I would be the most devoted, loving wife to my unsuspecting husband. I would sculpt my life and desires to just please him and spend my nights in his tender caressing arms and feel contentment. And soon, all of a sudden without warning I would be yearning for reckless Roger again. And when his arms grabbed me from the back and lay on me like a mindless beast, I would welcome him eagerly. My ears will be closed to remonstrations for holiness, my heart burn with lust. Oh this is tearing me apart...

I enjoyed watching Susan write her diary. Her poise, the sound of her pen scratching paper and the sigh she takes when ending a sentence, they all brought a sense of contentment to my soul.

"Husband, did you know that there are at some 350 million souls in China? In the short time that the Gospel was introduced, there have been 10 million souls saved! Isn't it incredible?"She asked one day. I was reading the San Francisco Herald, The Star's rival. The headline read 'Slavery in Chinatown – Highbinders and Slave-women - a tale of degradation.'

"Those are 350 million desperate souls. They'll believe anything. When the British brought them opium, 20 million souls gobbled it up." I found myself parroting Chen Ping, with whom I have lost touch for almost a decade.

"You are just pulling numbers out of the air. How do you know that?"

"I just do."

"You're not even Chinese."

"I am. Look." I showed her my hairless arm.

"Where's your Chinese passport? Where is your queue?"

"You're the only one I know who bothered with such dour details. In any case, you should be thankful I'm not. Or you would certainly have bound feet and I will be taking a second wife by now."

No smart response.

I nudged her.

"Eh?"

"Lee Seong, will you really take a second wife?" she asked quietly.

"I was only joking. No I will not."

"How about a concubine?"

"No, I couldn't afford one," I joked.

"Why do Chinese men want so many wives?"

"We don't. As a matter of fact, most Chinese men that I know do not. Like other cultures, having a lot of women is a sign of achievement and posterity. In cultures all over the world, the victorious king or general rewards himself with many women; and it was lauded by society. Monogamy is a fairly new and radical idea, propounded by Christianity only in recent times."

"Well, I think monogamy is what God wanted for Man."

"Father Abraham would disagree with you. Or King David; man after God's own heart. Or King Solomon, the wisest man on earth. Or..."

"Oh, shut up, Lee Seong."

"I am but just a simple Chinaman. Initially I set out to find a wife to satisfy my father's dying wish. Now I have a wife, a best friend, a better part of me and I need no one else."

A moment's silence.

"What about after I die?"

"What?

"Will you re-marry after I die?"

"What makes you think I'll let you die before me?"

"Just answer me."

"The Chinese believe a man and woman when bound by destiny are inseparable, like a pair of chopsticks. Even in the Underworld, life goes on as husband and wife. Death does not do us part. If I die first, I will merely wait for you. What does the Bible say about husbands and wives in the hereafter?"

"I don't know but I will ask Reverend Armstrong tomorrow."

"You trust that pretentious old coot too much." Ted Armstrong is the spiritual leader of the new church Susan has been going to since her marriage to me.

"Don't call him that. He's my spiritual adviser"

"He can advise you no more about the spirit world than I could tell you about China. He's full of fart, like Woods."

Susan giggled. The two Reverends did have ample girths and wheezed audibly when they talked.

"I still don't like the way you talk about him like that."

"I'm the Head of household, and I can do and say whatever I want in this house."

"Alright head of household, you haven't answered my question. Will you or not re-marry after I'm gone?"

I put down the newspaper and made a show of thinking deeply, putting my fist on my chin for emphasis.

"I will answer that tomorrow. Time to go to bed."

"As mistress of household I demand you answer it now!" she started to tickle me.

It was starting to get to me. She was up to something.

One day during Mid Autumn Festival, we were strolling in Chinatown. In those days, the only strollers in Chinatown were old maids hi-binders on patrol for their tongs. But it was Mid Autumn Festival, and homesickness could cast even the most venomous rivalry aside. Wealthy merchants decorated their shops with lanterns and calligraphy. It was a cool serene night. The streets were bright with lanterns and cacophony. Children were running in the streets. The sidewalks were lined with makeshift stalls. I have since stopped breaking out in a cold sweat after venturing a few steps out of Chinatown like I did for several years since returning from my wanderings after my university stint. Here, a place I grew up, although vilified by the rest of the country as a hellhole, not without reason was still a place I could still defend myself and Susan. Out there, though unlike the sojourners I could read the signs and understand the language, I could not even guarantee my own safety.

There is another reason I shun the outside world now.

When Susan conversed with other white males, she displayed a sense of casual ease. With me she was more intense, those bright blue eyes boring into my soul and tickling my heart. I found myself envying the boorish white men. They seemed to enjoy a side of Susan denied to me. There will come a day when I cease to be fascinating to her. The child-like curiosity will be dampened by familiarity. She would wake up and wonder why she was lying in bed with a

Chinaman. I trembled at such thoughts and wondered how I would react. Would I exercise violence? Or just break down like an effeminate male? Or would I easily move on to spend the remaining years of my life with a Chinese woman; as dictated by Heaven I should?

These were thoughts too terrible to behold. They broke into dust when I felt her squeeze my hand, to wake me from my ruminations, as she had guessed from my glazed stare; or I did not hear something she said.

Susan was dressed imperceptibly in a long Chinese gown and kept her brown hair covered in a dark fedora, looking simply resplendent, in my humble opinion. The ambience was festive. There's even an er-hu troupe playing; a haunting tune from my childhood that about the green hills of China. It was almost as if the violence and hardships of the day never existed. I received my salary that day and was eager to spend it. As I was peering over a stall to look for a nice anklet, she pulled me towards her.

With her sweetest smile, she said,

"Can I ask you for something?"

"I would give you the whole world and the moon, minus Chinatown," I smiled.

Instead of giggling, she grew somber.

"Husband, shall we go to China?"

I thought for a while.

"It is a dangerous time….." I smiled. She has always been fascinated by anything non-western.

"I felt a calling from God to live there."

"And how long does God want you to live there?" I asked cautiously.

"For the rest of my life."

"What?!"

We returned home quickly, as I was simmering.

"How long have you been harboring this intention?"

"Long before you came into my life. It was not an 'intention'. It is God's calling"

"You know that going to China and marrying a Chinese man are two quite different things?"

"I know!" he exclaimed in her petulant way. "Husband, if I hadn't met you, I would've gone to China years ago."

I felt betrayed. I slammed my palm on the table so hard it echoed across the room. Even after the echo died down and the pain shooting up my arm has subsided, the tension remained. Susan was visibly shocked at my reaction.

I've spent my whole adult life being fascinated with and dissociating from China I could not help but suspect that as though I was part of a package.

"Alright Susan. If I refuse to come with you, would you still go to China?"

She was quiet. For a little too long. Tears as big as raindrops rolled down her angular cheeks. I was biting back my own sorrow and anger.

"No," she said quietly.

Still feeling a nudging notion that my Susan could've married me to fulfill her missionary aspirations, I fell into a fitful sleep.

S's

Roger! The beast! This demon in man manifest!

We did it three more times after the first; each time I resisted less than the last. During each time I fantasized that Roger would just whisk me away and live in shame in some forgotten place. I knew it would not happe He is a cad. But God help me I could not resist him!

It all changed last week. After he had his way with me he turned around with the most sinister grin.

"Tell that Chinaman of yours that I want two hundred dollars. Else a certain adultery will be on every lips from Chinatown to Monterrey. Now my little pixie, these Mongols punish adultery by drowning em. Not as bad as being stoned to death. But your choice, love." And then that hateful man left. I don't know how long I cried, how I wish could hold on to Seong and tell him everything. China! I am afraid. It has taken much prayer to even think about it. If he does not agree then the only recourse is face my sins and the punishment that must one day come.

It will hurt him so. Perhaps he might kill me? I am so afraid. Lord forgive my sins; o my carnal sins! As I felt the last drops of human dignity seeped out of me, I got on my knees and begged Roger. I would sell all my possessions and he could have it just for him to spare Seong. He sneered and I would forever remember his last words before he dropped his cigarette on my neck.

"I want the money alright. But most of all my boots want their rightful place on top of a Chinaman's bitch."

"Hello, Mrs Lee." She smiled a groggily. I put my arm around her and gently drew circles onto a small circular mark on her nape. Susan woke up and purred, the previous night's discomfort forgotten.

"Let's go to China," I said.

No response.

She fell right back asleep in my arms.

Let's go to China.

Actually, it was a full 3 years before we actually board the ship to China. For all intents and purposes, we made preparations to spend the rest of our lives there.

The San Francisco Chinese Mission Board rejected her application twice. The first time around they cited that she would not be prepared for the most insurmountable difficulties.

During the second application she brought me along and introduced me as her husband to a committee of white old men, all of whom Susan looked highly upon. For my dear wife, I began with an oration about my dual-cultural background. The insurmountable difficulties faced by other missionaries were attributable to their foreign appearance and approach but it would easily be overcome by two of us as a team.

I wasn't quite prepared for their next line of questioning.

'Do you believe that Man is saved by believing in the Father, Son and Holy Ghost?' Yes

'Have I been baptized?' Yes

'How long have I been a practicing Christian?' more than five years

'Which is the most profound Bible verse I have encountered?' Thirteenth chapter of John, verse 15. I recited it.

'Please recite the Apostle's Creed'

I was unable to.

"But gentlemen, my wife would be the missionary; not I."

That was lost to them. They rejected Susan's application. I was secretly elated.

Then a letter came. It was a tearful appeal from the Morrison team in Guangzhou for more money, manpower and prayer, read to the congregation by a haggard missionary later pleaded to be sent to Africa rather than back to China. The letter also mentioned that the translation of the Chinese Bible and other materials is making progress but has been hampered by the lack of bi-linguists. Susan marched up the Mission committee and made it clear to them she would go to China with or without their blessing. They relented. I moved back to preparation mode.

I wrote a request a letter to my good friend Sebastian Chow who was now in Hong Kong to secure an insurance. As well, for the first time in my life, I started to shave my forehead. Now at that time, 'Bucktooth Song still had his barber corner at the end of Grant Avenue. Bucktooth Lee deserved a mention here. Prior to the earthquake, he was the most respected man in Chinatown. Unlike Old Master Lee or Hwang, no one feared Bucktooth Lee. He operated a makeshift stall towards the rear end of Chinatown where he provided herbalism, acupuncture and barbering services to all, young and old, wealthy and poor, high-binder or miner alike and charged everyone the same nominal fee. New arrivals, children, the homeless were charged nothing. In fact, rumor had it that his was the only stall untouched by the tongs' protection racket. His only detractor was Blind Man Kung, as Bucktooth Lee often lectured his customers on the perils of superstitions when inquired for 'high knowledge'. His 'stall' was really a decrepit makeshift chamber with a wooden roof with enough room for him and a stool for the customer. When I requested him for a shave to grow a queue, his shorted sighted eyes squinted at me

"Young brother, you don't need to grow a queue," he said simply and turned his back.

"I am going home," I explained.

"I know. That is why this is would be more useful instead," he chuckled, revealing his namesake. From a drawer he took out a hat with a queue attached to it.

"You are going to China for the first time in your life. This can pass a casual inspection. Besides you need more than a queue to explain yourself to your family for bringing home a foreign bride," he said.

I was startled. He could not possibly have known. Was it Old Hwang? He started laughing.

"Don't' worry your secret is safe with me young brother. And those who know your secret have kept it to themselves as well."

"But how--?" I asked

But Bucktooth Song kept silent, smiling his secret smile.

"And they say Blind Kung is a fairy from heaven. I'd say Bucktooth Lee is a demigod!" I declared, to egg him on.

"Such stupidity for a son of the Yellow Emperor," he admonished, his smile turned to a scowl. He took a deep sigh. "Your stiff gait tells me either you have a love disease on your penis or you've been wearing foreigners' costume for a while; at least their stiff trousers and hard shoes."

"The ink stains on the inner side of your palm," he continued, "could not have been from calligraphy. You have been writing horizontally, not the natural way."

Then he lowered his voice. "That womanly whiff from your shirt is a pungent aroma from an oil-based substance mixed with lavender, rose, sandalwood and two more ingredients unknown to me. Only Old Hwang's wives and the foreigners use it."

"Lastly," he said with a hidden smile at my astonished look." Your upper body is straight. Arms are stringy, with the hands of woman. Your hips are airy, with thighs that have never sustained more than your own body weight. And your cheeks are full and bright. You've never done hard labor but possess some means. You are a scholar; but not of Confucious."

I was amazed. I was in the presence of a wise man. Truly, he deserved his other moniker, the 'Oracle of Outside China.'

"I have no more words for you, young brother," he suddenly lost interest. "Go away."

I paid for the queue and thanked him.

"We will meet again," he ended cryptically.

I digressed. With my queue attached, I took a long hard look at the mirror and couldn't recognize the man in there. There I was, a subject of the emperor, a sign of subservience and weakness. Absence of a queue in China was apparently capital punishment. A strong and stable civilization need not base its identity on so flimsy an item. The more romantic sojourners described it as a loyalty to an emperor I neither knew nor care. I saw a man strangled to death with his own queue during a street fight in Chinatown, and many a times the sight of a Chinaman being pulled about like an animal by his queue made me hate it. My father wore a queue all his life but never made me wear one. I've always wondered why. Now looking at myself like a mirror image of my father, I understood. Lee Kau was not a sojourner. He was an immigrant. He never intended for me to go back to China.

"Hello handsome."

Susan came in.

"Look what I've transformed into. I hope you're happy," still looking at the mirror, my back towards her.

"Ohh...how delightful," (she said it with a high inflection) "It does make me feel...somewhat flustered," she cooed, hitting a high tone with the last word.

She hugged me from the back and ran her fingers down my abdomen until she reached my crotch.

My wife's like that.

The rest of the time in the three years, I continued working at The Star, keeping a low profile but reaching further and further in my influence. Meanwhile Susan attended her 'missionary classes' learning basic medical practice, midwifery, preaching, and so forth. She was always so joyous; an inexhaustible reservoir from whence I draw my own sustenance.

1953

Writing one's memoir is tiring work. I wish I had started when I was a younger man.

I just remembered something. I haven't seen it for a while. Have I lost it?

No not in the trousers pockets. No not in my shirt pocket. No not in jackets either!

Where can it be? Keep calm now Lee Seong. Where did you last felt it?

Was it last night that you kept on the drawer on the bed? Or was it 10 years ago in Salinas? You old fool Lee Seong!

How can you be so reckless!

Where can it be?! Ah...there you are, just next to the inkstand all this while.

I caressed the precious object, a faded jade engraved with the character 'Snow'

It was a gloomy morning in November 1886 when Susan and I boarded a Singapore bound steamer to begin life in a foreign land. Rose Milton actually came to see us off. She exchanged kisses and a tearful goodbye with Susan but had no words for me. Nonetheless we stayed on the stern and waved goodbye until the pier was out of sight.

Onboard the ship, the Caucasians and Orientals were set apart; unless you had a first-class private cabin; which was what we purchased. Still, I wore my queue, kept my head down and made sure I walked three steps behind Susan, lest unwanted attention was aroused. Occasionally, we had to venture out for nature calls, refreshments or fresh air. Once when I was trying to trade with another passenger for some herbs for Susan, I spied a white man in his 50s with a groomed beard and monocles approaching her on the Caucasian deck. They conversed. He became quite animated and laid his hand on hers; causing her to withdraw quickly.

That did it. I launched the packet of herbs I was holding across the deck. It had luo han guo in it, which had shells as hard as rocks. It hit him straight across the face. His monocles fell right out. I quickly ran forward retrieve it.

"Oh! Soli muchee! Soli muchee!" while making gestures it was some unseen culprits from around the corner.

I bent over to pick it up and disappeared.

Susan also took the opportunity to escape.

Back in the cabin, she was laughing uncontrollably, spilling her herbal tea.

"If he touches you like that again I will kill him."

"Seong! You are a Christian!"

"No, me evil pig-tailed Chinaman. Don't make Chinaman angry. Chinaman kill!"

She laughed again and laid her head on my chest lovingly.

Other than that, it was an uneventful journey. The port at Singapore was a fascinating collation of sights and smells. Between me and her prayers, Susan took in everything as happy as a child. In contrast I was constantly worried about us and kept looking at our backs in case of any assailant from either race. Letters from Brother Robinson were especially foreboding. Anti-British or rather, anti-Caucasian sentiments were conflagrant. Thus, it was not a surprise when our ship's captain decided not to risk it and turned away from Canton port to dock at Macao instead; which suited me fine. I left Susan at the Macao Evangelistic Mission to acquire information about Canton while I went in search of my old friend and mentor. The Macao La Salle Mission School for Boys was extraordinary stone building of Portuguese architecture, standing amidst the slum houses surrounding it. I was surprised that the address Brother Robinson gave me was to a more modest house standing next to it.

Brother Robinson came out running.

"Seong-y boy!" He gave me a bear hug and tugged at my queue.

"This is real?"

"As real as my person."

He nodded perceptively. Brother Robinson understood sarcasm.

"Brother Robinson,"

"Just Peter Robinson," he corrected me.

"I left the fraternity. I got married," he grinned. "She's what the future would call 'Eurasian'. She's out at the market now. I'm just a teacher now; Chinese history." He laughed at his own irony.

"Come on in!"

Inside Brother Robinson's cool colonial style home and over hot tea, I told him about Susan.

"So that's what caused the change!" he exclaimed, gesturing at my queue, followed by the uproarious laugh. "I know you didn't come to China just to visit old Pete here; nor to spread the Good News. Only a woman can make a man do the things he doesn't want to do."

His brow furrowed when he heard about our plans.

"So, you're really a Christian now?"

I shrugged.

"Ah, married to a missionary. Was it for love?"

I affirmed vehemently.

"What a peculiar tale. Someone ought to be writing down your story. Look Seongy, I tried to live in Guangzhou for a while. It was impossible. That god-forsaken city was chaotic. The government absolutely forbids almost any activity by foreigners; even if it were just the kung fu guilds and the mob that executes these laws. It's like San Francisco; except the table's turned against the whites. Mostly it was the damn British fault, what the opium and all. If I were you, take a nice safari up north to Beijing or Nanjing; then get the hell out of China."

Deep down in me, I agreed with every word as I shook my head smiling.

When we bade farewell. Peter Robinson became tearful.

"In Chinatown I was so, so lonely. I couldn't stand the rednecks and the Chinese didn't want anything to do with me; even when I spoke Chinese. You were my only friend."

I gave him a parting gift; a 4th edition of the translated Count of Monte Christo.

After that I returned to the Mission to retrieve Susan. The missionaries there echoed what Brother Robinson told me and advised against going to Canton. She was crestfallen. Her sadness weighed upon my heart like an anchor does to a ship.

"Susan, we will go to Canton."

She looked at me quizzically.

"We need to get information from the horse's mouth, don't we? Besides, there's someone I want you to meet."

The land of the dragon

The road journey from Macao to Canton was most unnerving. Aside from the fact we did not have Brother Robinson's blessing (his tearful farewell was in stark contrast to when he bade me goodbye at the San Francisco pier all those years ago.) His sweaty palm, tear streaked face and hollow eyes suggested that we would never meet again. I was in completely foreign territory. We travelled in coach used only by foreigners; my masquerade as a Chinese servant getting less welcome the deeper, we travelled into Guangdong. Cities that we passed by were no more different than Chinatown. The disparity between the destitute and the aristocratically wealthy was apparent. Beggars and old-looking young men in service were ubiquitous. It was very much like Chinatown in San Francisco. The tranquil and esthetic China that Chinatown sojourners so often spoke of likely existed only in their minds.

"Ah Yee!"

Every coolie in the rice warehouse turned to see who just greeted their Old Master with such a familiar term. Ah Yee turned around with the brightest of smile. Except for an extra furrow or two on his forehead and a trimmed moustache, my childhood child hadn't changed a bit. Suddenly seemingly out of nowhere, a man started to approach me with a drawn sword. With my hair bristling, I drew Susan behind me. Ah Yee placed a hand on the swordsman's shoulder and signaled him away. Then he turned to us beaming. Sporting a beard and wearing a distinguished silk jacket, he clasped my hand tightly.

"Please excuse Ah Jian, he's a newly hired bodyguard. There have been some thefts at the warehouse recently," he apologized. "Ah, the beautiful Mrs. Lee, true to testimony. I'm charmed," he said in English.

Susan blushed at the compliment.

"Your English hasn't left you," I marveled, which was true with the exception of a mild hint of Chinese accent.

"Plenty of opportunities to practice here, as you probably noticed. Come on in!" he invited heartily. My heart felt as if it would burst at the sight of my old friend and adopted brother.

We were introduced to his three children. Ah Yee's Fujian cook made all of Old Ma's dishes of my childhood. It was a sumptuous dinner. Before long, I began to ease. Ah Yee's wife looked like an old hand in playing the gracious hostess. She does not speak any English but seemed eager to communicate with Susan with a mixture of pidgin, hand gestures and smiles. She broke yelps of joy when Susan spoke Cantonese. I was overjoyed to see my old friend so settled and well. We could not wait to hear each other's stories but mutually understood it was not conversations for the womenfolk and servants around the dinner table. Ah Yee's face darkened when he heard about Susan's missionary aspirations.

"You could not have come to China at a worse time. Forget the Chinese people. Let us work out our own salvation."

Susan was dumbstruck and then came familiar flashing of her eyes caused me to quickly place my hands on hers under the table. I noticed from his trembling chopstick gestures, Ah Yee was struggling to control himself.

"I think we should we bring our guests to visit our famed pottery in Foshan," Ah Yee's wise wife changed the topic.

"A good idea" I quickly concurred.

That night, with the women downstairs, Ah Yee and I were sitting on his opulent verandah; with a gourd of lip-smacking ng kar pi and smoking pipes. The warm crisp of warm Guangdong attracting all manner of night insects symphonizing in the dark.

"I'm sorry I was rude just now," he said

I brushed him off.

"What's troubling you Ah Yee? I know you've been through hardship but you seemed to have 'arrived'" I said, gesturing at the wealth before us.

"When I was growing up, papa wanted us to be successful in Chinatown. He brought every single family member there. He even engaged an English tutor for that purpose. It was as if he never intended to return to China."

"You can't blame him. Old Master was a success story in Chinatown, revered by many."

Ah Yee pondered that.

"Perhaps that was true," he continued. "When we were first driven out of my mother's family, I worked at a number of odd jobs; one of which was as a kitchen hand in a westerners' club- A place in China where Chinese were not allowed to enter. They did not know that I understood them. While I was cleaning their tables and scrubbing their floors, I heard so much nasty, scornful things about out people. The mockery, the insults distressed me. Throughout my childhood, papa has shielded us from this sad reality. They were all out to rob us! And China is a nation on her knees! And her people are leaving her in droves! At her greatest time of need! You asked me if I was bitter that Ah Yat drove us out of Chinatown. I hadn't been sure of the answer but I can confidently tell you that I am thankful to him; for opening my eyes to the world at large. My father spent his life fighting for a few filthy streets in Chinatown. But here, here I now know that there is a fight for a whole nation!" Although it did not sound like he delivered this speech for the first time, Ah Yee was still visibly incensed, tobacco ash spilling out from his pipe onto his trembling hands.

"And the religion that your wife brings to us; I believe all religion started out to be good, but here, they've used it to subjugate us; made us weak. They tore down our ancestral temples and built their churches. They disrespected our Emperor and trampled on our culture!"

I sipped my tea, and kept silent.

"Have you heard of the Rebellion of the Long Haired Robbers?"

I admitted I had not.

"It was a civil war that happened a few years before we were born. It almost tore this country apart. After that, the foreigners forced the Emperor to make concessions and gave them land that they have now."

I was filled with admiration for the passion exuding from my old childhood friend. The energy shone in his eyes. He looked years younger than his age and projected an aura of command much brighter than the one his father had. His words sparked a flame within me. But my only vision of the future was one in which Susan and I are together.

"What do you plan to do?" I asked.

"I don't know. The Imperial Court is at its weakest and is no match for a military showdown with the foreign powers. China's greatest strength is her youths and we are all mobilized. A peasant revolt seemed inevitable; but against the white devils, they will be slaughtered. Inevitably, the decisive action will be an all-out war."

Such talk caused goose bumps to form all over my skin.

"War?" I uttered helplessly.

"Seong, you were always the most scholarly amongst us. You even went to university in the West! The New China will need the likes of you."

"Well old friend," I began, searching my mind for an appropriate, appeasing statement. "Like you mentioned, China's greatest assets are us Chinamen. And in hundred years, we will still prevail."

Ah Yee drew long on his pipe and sighed; leaving many words unspoken. "I would give up all my possessions to see that day." He understood and did not push further.

The next few weeks we spent with Ah Yee's family were uneventful and blissful. His wife brought us to see spectacular sights in the countryside. Throughout our visit however, I could sense that Ah Yee was constantly troubled. He snapped at his children and decidedly ignored Susan. I decided that we have overstayed out welcome.

The next morning we travelled to the Baptist Mission but found the church's door was locked. Crossed with yellow papers that state 'Down with Foreign Cults!' Guangdong was a nexus of chaos. Chinese and westerners lived in a state of constant tension and fear much more palpable than Chinatown. While sojourners kept their heads down and avoided confrontation whenever possible, Guangdong locals openly defied the well-armed, well protected westerners. Amongst the westerners, though mostly were British, there were also Germans, French, Portuguese and a handful of Americans; none of whom shared President Cleveland's aspiration for foreigners to assimilate into the society in which they adopted. The unpredictable political climate, dusty streets, hostile environment all made it extremely unsavory for me. It didn't help that it was raining every day while we were there.

Susan seemed unperturbed.

"God will start a great revival here amongst the Chinese," she predicted firmly.

I had my doubts about that but kept my thoughts to myself.

What eventually sealed Susan's evangelistic aspirations was not my coddling, neither was it Ah Yee's matter-of-fact outburst. It was someone who came with us all the way from California.

Susan was pregnant.

S's

I thank the Lord for this second chance in life. I will take my secret sins to my grave and face the Maker in my shame. But I will not sully my husband's name as long as he is alive. I now know what it means to love someone unconditionally. Oh how I hate the Susan of San Francisco. Not a day goes by that I do not curse the woman.

The streets are filthy. The people wore hostile glances. But this was the first time after a long while that my heart and my soul was at peace.

I cried and sobbed silently when Seong made love to me, that after I've done, I still have someone to love me. Chinese women are so stoic, yet steadfastly loyal to their husbands, treating them as masters. O how much my Seong deserves them. I am such a disgrace. Many a times I pondered upon the lake and thought of ending it all.

Poor Seong possess a completely misguided impression of me. For once, finally, I will be Seong's Susan, and by God I will actually be happy.

And it wasn't an easy pregnancy. For the first two months she threw up everything she ate and was constantly nauseous every morning. For some reason she begun craving rye bread. Bread in China! Luckily, the British Club in the

International Settlement had some; and agreed to send some to Mr. Buzz after a handsome tip was promised.

"you bling de bleaddd? Tankee kew veli muchee. Mr Buss not home. Here, monee now. Goode bye!"

I slammed the door and fed my poor Susan, who could not even rise from the bed.

"You both should leave China immediately," Ah Yee said firmly when I told him of Susan's pregnancy.

"I agree, but Susan's in no shape for the journey," I protested.

"Look, something's about to happen here," Ah Yee said, his voice trailing off. I understood and did not press further.

"Alright, go to my mother's ancestral home in the countryside. Right now. I'll hire an ox-cart. Just pack the necessities. I'll send word ahead that you are my kin."

It was a grueling slow four hour ox cart journey into the Guangzhou hinterland, with Susan throwing up every half hour or so. She looked so pale I thought she would die.

We settled in a rural place in Guangzhou. A village of about fifty souls.

It was an abandoned house on Ah Yee's wife's ancestral plot; a doorless, gateless stone house with an intact roof. In the hall was a simple wood coffin which was fortunately empty. Miraculously, Susan stopped vomiting the day after we moved in.

The pristine countryside and simple folks reminded me that this were the origins of my father, Old Ma, Old Master

Lee.

I spent my days pretending to be a Chinese peasant. And I liked it. For the first time, the horrors of Chinatown and Guangzhou seemed so far away.

The money we brought from America could go such a long way here I even took up painting to while away the time. But Susan was restless. She provided classes to the local children.

"The Lord sent us here to save souls. Not enjoy the countryside!"

"Hush now, you know the city is no place for the baby."

"I haven't distributed a single pamphlet since we've been here. Not a single soul."

"Be patient. The Lord works in mysterious ways."

She had no reply to that. I pulled her close and caressed her abdomen. Privately, I anticipated with glee the blissful life ahead.

"Do you suppose our child will be a boy or girl?" I asked putting my head to her belly, feeling for the first quickening.

"I would want a boy first; but what would you like, my master of the household?" she asked, caressing my shaved head, of which I was still self-conscious about.

"A girl, actually. What kind of features do you suppose she will have?"

Once a month, we would travel to Guangzhou by cart to get supplies and also news of the current situation. It was a beautiful morning as the ox-cart travelled slowly across the earthen road. Sorghum wheat was growing healthily for as far as the eye could see. Our journey was serenade by the birds of spring. There was a thin cloud of mist where the ancients reside. The air was cool. And the sky was a masterpiece of blue and yellow hue with celestial clouds. Except for the occasional water buffalo, not a soul was in sight. If not for sharp cloppity- clop of the ox, I would be forgiven to imagine we were in heaven.

Susan's cheeks were flushed pink like a Northerner. She was reading her ever-present diary; and a dictionary she was compiling on new phrases, smiling to herself, no doubt eager to work on it once we arrived.

"What are you thinking about?"

She just smiled.

We borrowed the ox cart from our farmer neighbor who absolutely resisted all kinds of payment.

"Just make sure you buy from the city a lot of nutritious food for Snow Mountain. Write this down so you can remember!" the old woman insisted as she ranted on the herbs and ingredients needed for Susan's 'pregnancy soup', a pungent broth reminiscent of Old Ma.

For the past two months, Susan was well loved and cared for by the village like a princess.

We left the ox-cart at the care of a farm by the city outskirts and walked in. The pregnancy was having a toll on Susan's back. She wore a scarf to cover her features and the heavily padded jacket of a country peasant. Her Cantonese was almost flawless now with only a tinge of accent.

"Husband, I will go the Bible Mission to check for news."

"Alright, just let me…"

"No, don't come with me. Go shop so we could leave earlier. I'm a little unwell today." She did seem a bit pale to me.

It was a humid day. The dusty roads of Canton made the heat uncomfortable. The salty breeze from the sea tasted sour with the ships at the dock, their merchandise and human sweat. There were the usual sick people on the streets, numerous beggars and occasional scuffle. Bustling, cacophonic and busy, it was not unlike any other day at the port city. Of course, at that time I was only thinking of my joy and the serene countryside as I watched Susan's back. Just as she disappeared from view, suddenly there was a burst of guns and the neigh of horses. The beasts appeared apparently from nowhere onto the marketplace. Their riders wore black, with a red scarf over their heads and armed with swords. People ran helter-skelter. Some jumped into the sea. It was not long before the crates by the pier and the docked ships were torched, sending up columns of evil black smoke.

I just witnessed the opening shots and the first of many skirmishes of what would the western press refer as the Boxer Rebellion. The horses kicked dust up, choking nostrils and burning eyes. Women were screaming.

Amidst the chaos I yelled for Susan.

Chinese civilians were running from the Redscarves. One of them pulled me off the main street to safety. But he wouldn't let go. I turned around and punched him in the face. Once liberated, I ventured out to the main street. Smoke and gunpowder smell was everywhere. I noticed Susan amidst the rubble by her ash-brown hair. I quickly pulled her to safety and noticed the abandoned ox-cart still by the roadside.

I carried Susan over to the cart, covered her with hay and straw and started to whip the beast to fly.

In what seemed to be endless hours, the cart reached the city gate. It was manned by government troops. I was not sure to feel relief or fear. My cart was stopped and before the soldiers bayoneted the cart, I quickly exposed the hay to find my Susan perspiring and breathing heavily. Her headscarf was missing.

"Please brother, she is my wife," I implored. "We are heading back to the village."

At this, the soldiers burst out laughing.

"Sure she is. Off with you. Don't tire yourself out now you dirty peasant." With that, they laughed uproariously.

I wasted no time and put myself at the mercy of the ox and his guardian spirit to take us back to the village. I whipped, pleaded, scolded and even pulled the ears of the beast to hurry up, checking on Susan intermittently. She seemed mildly responsive but did laugh at my panicky antics. The cart sank into mud. With seeming impossible strength, I lifted it up and released my woman, cart and beast.

Then to my horror, the cart was stained with blood. The sun has set by the time I arrived back at the village. I yelled for the old woman in the village. She came with her broad-shouldered daughter in-law and they helped carry Susan into the house and barked out orders at me.

Susan's tears fell, breaking my heart with each drop.

By nightfall, the old woman emerged from the house.

"She needs to rest. But you should go in," she said gently.

"The child..?"

She shook her head.

"It is God's will, His test for us. We must not lose faith, my husband," Susan said with closed eyes, praying. Her breathing was labored.

The old woman brought us food, which I gratefully accepted.

While Susan rested in the adjoining room, I stared in the darkness, mourning our child. The candle on the table top went out. My exhausted mind searched frantically for ways to bring Susan back into the city safely, where the hospitals are. As it was approaching midnight, there was a banging on the door. It was loud to convey urgency but not enough to wake the neighbors.

I opened the door and to my surprise, there stood Ah Yee; his clothes stained in mud. He was panting heavily, sweat dripping down his face.

"Oh brother, you need to this place now. I don't know why..." he was struggling to catch his breath.

"What are you talking about?"

"Ah Jian! He's not my bodyguard. He's a chieftain with The Righteous Fist Society. He came to my warehouse that day to ask for support." Tears were flowing down his eyes. His spectacles were askew. I could hardly recognize the man before me.

"The uprising in the city today," he continued. "It was a bloodbath. Government troops declared war and many brothers died. The remnant group has sworn revenge on all foreigners and Chinese abetting foreigners. Ah Jian came to me, asking for you. He wanted to kill you both the moment you came to my house."

I was in shock.

"I don't know why I did it!" he blurted. "The brotherhood, the patriotism, they all made so much sense!"

I just had to ask. "You betrayed me? So you told that killer where to find me and my wife? Did you know I just lost my child today?"

Ah Yee's face went pale as a ghost.

Oh, Seong I'm so sorry! I'm so sorry!" he exclaimed over and over again.

For the second time in my life, I punched a man right in the face and sent him flying.

Ah Yee stood up, wiped the blood from his nose and said firmly,

"You need to leave now!"

Without another word, I burst into the adjoining room and reached Susan. She was awake, barely conscious but heard everything that transpired. She moved her lips barely.

"Let us go, husband."

It was too late. The dark horizon was lit with torches. Shouts of men were heard, of various accents I could not recognize. They were getting louder with every second. I slipped out the back of the house and ran towards the horizon, into the sorghum fields, without direction. Susan became exceedingly weak. I carried her on my back. The sound of her panting down my neck nudged me onAs I ran, I tried to understand the reasoning behind us being hunted down like animals. Images of the hollow men from Wyoming sped across my mind; as well as of my own father as he ran for his life with his wife on his back. Like them, I was running away from insanity, violence, desperation and fellow men. Men who hunt down strangers as enemies. Will we ever escape them? And why is my wife getting lighter? To my horror, the lower part of her skirt began to feel warm and wet. She had begun bleeding again.

I ran like there was no tomorrow, into the sorghum fields. I felt no fatigue. I wasn't sure if our pursuers were still at our backs but I was running out of China; across her vast abdomen back to her shores and out of her borders. When I dared to turn around, I saw in the distance figures of men with weapons drawn and lit torches. This made me sprint faster. I only stopped when I heard Susan breathed into ear, softly and weakly.

"Husband, stop."

There was a large pool of blood all over Susan's abdomen and my arms, some dried; most fresh. I cradled her in my arms. The dawning sky was mockingly calm. There was a pile of blood emanating from her abdomen. I put my hand to apply pressure to stop it. Within seconds, her blood enveloped my hand. Her still body feeling colder as time passed. I tried the kiss of life, the repositioning of her qi.

"Susan, stay with me," I said in English my vision hazed with tears.

"Husband," she replied in Cantonese."I'm sorry, so sorry."

"Don't say that...hush now, please don't say that!"

Her lips became the color of her skin.

With a burst of strength, my beloved Susan raised her hand up to touch my chin and then she reached into her pocket and retrieved her diary. The last page stained quickly with blood read:

The beautiful person's like a flower beyond the edge of the clouds. Above is the black night of heaven's height; Below is the green water billowing on. The sky is long, the road is far, bitter flies my spirit; The spirit I dream can't get through, the mountain pass is hard. Long yearning, Breaks my heart. 2

And then she was no more.

I spent the whole day and night in the field motionless with Susan's body. First I beseeched the gods of China for a miracle. Then I cursed them for their violence and inhumanity. I cursed Ah Yee. I cursed China. After that I bargained with Jesus. Susan had given Him all the good years of her life, at least let me have some more of her. But just like the Chinese gods, he remained deaf to my pleas. The remainder of the night, amidst the sounds of the wild I spoke to Susan, all the things I was going to tell her in the rest of our lifetime together. When dawn broke I was certain I was going to go insane.

The sudden craving for human company and civilization knocked me out of my grief. I retraced my steps back to the village; half hoping the rebels were still there to finish me off. It was another a day and half when I at last collapsed at the front door of Susan's midwife. By this time, Susan's body has stiffened and begged to be laid to rest. The kindly old woman and her daughter in-law mourned with me. We buried her with my stillborn child in the village. We used the empty coffin in Ah Yee's ancestral home. Her gravestone bore a cross and inscribed in Chinese her name Lee Shu Shan, Mrs Lee Seong born 1854; died 1885 survived by Mr Lee Seong; followed by her favorite Psalm. I learned that the old woman and her daughter in-law were my true benefactors. They were awakened that morning by rage-filled Redscarves. Thinking on their feet, they pointed us out in the opposite direction. They did not see Ah Yee.

My grief was beyond description. For the next few months I was completely imprisoned within the despair and lost my senses and all reason. I spent the days by her graveside talking to her as though still alive. I did not starve to death solely by virtue of the kindness of the old woman and her daughter in-law Xiao Ping.

Months passed, one day as I stood in front of Susan's grave I was overcame with loneliness and loss and broke down. I wept for hours, my tears rolling down her gravestone mixed with the rain that came. The sun has set by the time I shuffled home, in a daze; drenched in rainwater and despondency. The food that Xiao Ping laid on the table has gone cold. After feebly attempting to force two grains of rice into mouth, my stomach revolted with disgust. I lay on the bunk and closed my eyes. The door opened and let in the bright moon light, which was brightest at the time Xiao Ping would come into the house to collect the dishes. I pretended to sleep.

She did not leave. Instead, I felt her body sitting next to mine. Our eyes met. She put her hands on my groin and began to caress. Xiao Ping's calloused hands were like butterflies dancing on my skin. Wordless, her gentle kneading and fondling made me aroused.

Desperate to detect a hint of Susan, I tore off her clothes hungrily and buried my face in her breasts, from which seem to emanate Susan's familiar scent. Xiao Ping remained wordless but pliable. She did not help with my undressing but made sure I know she wasn't against it. When I entered her and felt her body shudder, a thick fog lifted from my mind and I could feel my own life once more.

The next morning, I was at Canton Harbor. With Susan's bloodied letter and brooch in my pocket, I booked the first steamer to San Francisco.

At the port of entry, San Francisco,

"Hey you, Chinaman! Off to Angel Island."

I was rudely yanked out of the queue for 'Arrivals'

I smiled a toothy grin

"sor-ree sair. vely vely important letter for big boss," I took out my insurance from Sebastian Chow. The guard understood and I was led to see his supervisor.

"What's this now?"

It was a letter embossed with the words:

State Department of the United States of America

This hereby certifies Mr. Lee Seong is an American citizen and should be accorded all rights as such.

Signed

Thomas F. Bayard

Secretary of State

Where'd you get this letter, Chinaman?"

"You recognize the seal of the office bearer and I believe the letter was signed by Mr. Bayard. Now if you would kindly expedite my processing. My consul is waiting for me."

There was no Chinese Consul in San Francisco of course. Instead I hiked back to familiar grounds and crossed into the invisible barrier that enclosed a group of hated, mocked and despised people; my home. Back in Chinatown, my old friend Loneliness came running at my like an eager puppy. And when he engulfed me, he turned into Sorrow, the ugly witch. I simply could not bear to live in our apartment anymore. Looking back upon my life, the only time I was happy without Susan was when I was at the Lee Mansion; living as a servant.

I scoured the newspapers until I saw the ad I was looking
for. The next day, with my yet unpacked suitcase, I went to
the coach counter and said,
·escusee me, 1 ticket for the Sa-lee-nas velli plea see·
1953, San Francisco
And so began my quiet life in the valley. Ingratiating
myself into my employer·s family affairs affords me a
luxurious departure from my memories. The life of Lee
Seong is but a symphony of tragedy.

Maladies

Lee Kau suffered and died of consumption, a disease later renamed tuberculosis, a communicable disease caused by Mycobaterium tuberculosis. Pulmonary involvement causes chronic cough and a wasting syndrome. Invariably fatal without antibiotics and a major cause of death in the 19th century.

Lee Kau·s mother·s seizures were caused by metastatic cancer to the brain. Primary tumor was of the breast.

The Zheng family was afflicted by Brugada Syndrome; a genetic disease caused by mutations in the cellular makeup of cardiac cells that cause sudden death in young men by way of ventricular arrhythmias.

Old Ma·s sightings of ghosts were as a result of Charles Bonnet Syndrome. Sufferers experience complex visual hallucinations due to visual impairment.

Old Master Lee suffered from a fairly quick onset of Parkinsonism; characterized by slow shuffling gait, resting tremor and bradyphonia

Old Master Hwang towards the end developed alcoholic liver cirrhosis and a severe case of podagra.

Syphilis Hung indeed had syphilis. Neurosyphilis affecting the temporal lobes may manifest personality and behavioral changes, such as aggression, hypersexuality and loss of impulse control.

Blind Man Kung·s atrophied leg was due to poliomyelitis, a common disease of the nervous system in the 19th century. It is caused by the poliovirus

Peach Blossom·s son died of infant botulism; recognized only in the 20th century to be caused by toxins released by Clostridium botulinum; found exclusively in honey.

Little Emily likely succumbed to acute lymphoblastic lymphoma; a cancer that primarily affects children.

Susan experienced some degree of hyperemesis gravidarum early in her pregnancy.

Lee Seong has pectus excavatum, a congenital abnormality of the chest wall.

References

Poem by Yuan Zhen (779-831). Translated by Tony
Barnstone and Chou Ping Chinese Erotic Poems.
Everyman·s Library 2007
Long Yearning by Li Bai (701-762)

About the Author

Ernie Yap is originally from Malaysia, of Chinese
heritage. While in medical school, he survived crippling
poverty by working as a freelance writer for a couple of print
and online media in Malaysia, Canada and the United States.
He did book reviews, short stories and non-fiction.
His first attempt at a novel was titled RAMA which
now lies fallow on his desktop.
LEE is his second attempt.

9 7989 9 3 6 9 2 2 0 3